MILLIE

a novel by Peter Hargitai

iUniverse, Inc.

New York Lincoln Shanghai

MILLIE

Copyright © 2006 by Peter Hargitai

iUniverse books may be ordered through booksellers or by contacting:

iUniverse
2021 Pine Lake Road, Suite 100
Lincoln, NE 68512
www.iuniverse.com
1-800-Authors (1-800-288-4677)

Cover art by Thomas P. Muhl: "Leo the Cat"
Oil on canvas 30x36 in.
www.muhlpix.com

The publication of this book was made possible by support from the FIG Program at Florida International University

ISBN-13: 978-0-595-39920-8 (pbk)
ISBN-13: 978-0-595-84308-4 (ebk)
ISBN-10: 0-595-39920-7 (pbk)
ISBN-10: 0-595-84308-5 (ebk)

Printed in the United States of America

"Behold a shiny warrior on his horse,
Armed with tongues of flame,
Born of thunder and the stars,
See how he holds its shaggy mane,
How he blows the poet's horn."

—Aleksander Pushkin
"Ruslan and Lyudmilla"
(trans. Peter Hargitai)

CHAPTER 1

It was my first week as a college freshman at Cleveland State University. My Scientific German prof called my name out in class. Was there a Mr. Art Nagy in the room?

The professor said there was someone outside the door who wanted to see me.

A man wearing a suit and one of those new Afro hair-cuts said he was Detective Johnson from the Fairview Park Police Department. He wanted me to go with him down to the station. It was a matter of a few questions they wanted to ask about a certain neighborhood girl. I may want to take my books and stuff since there was a chance I wouldn't be back.

I was pretty rattled, but I pretended not to give a shit. So—I was caught. Finally.

The suburban police station was housed in an important-looking building on Lorain Avenue. The Stars and Stripes rippled against a bright-blue sky, the aluminum flagpole gleamed in the sun, everything was neat and clean.

I was told to sit down in front of a gray metal desk. Sergeant Lang would be with me shortly. Sergeant Lang took his sweet old time. Because after 20 minutes I was still waiting. My hands were sweating. I stared at the wall. A group picture of a Jaycees Little League team, glossy color photographs of the assassinated President John F. Kennedy and his successor, Lyndon B. Johnson.

It wasn't that long ago that I was staring at another wall with larger than life pictures of Lenin, Stalin and Marx. That was before the Hungarian Revolution and dodging Russian bullets to get to America. I felt bad for all the crud I got myself into since being here in the good old U.S. of A. I felt real bad for Millie. It was like one life ended in '56 with the Hungarian Revolution and another began with Millie in '65 when we vowed never to abandon each other.

How could I let things get to this far? I never told anyone, and now I was going to have to tell my life story to total strangers. A freaking detective of all people. The things is, I could never talk to my father. Maybe the fact that he was a judge had something to do with it. God, it was a weird year.

It started with the summer of '64. The summer of "I Walk the Line" by Johnny Cash and "Ticket to Ride" by the Beatles. The summer of the XVIII Olympiad in Tokyo and Hungarian gold in soccer. The summer of the 1964 Civil Rights Act. The summer we moved from the inner city to the suburbs of Fairview Park, Ohio. It was the summer before I met Millie. It was also the summer my Aunt Piroshka died.

I was pretty angry for having to transfer schools. I had been going to a Catholic all-boys school taught by the Brothers of Mary or Marionists as they called themselves. Oh yeah, this was also the year of the Warrior. That was the mascot of my new school, Fairview freaking High. My parents had me transfer to this crappy school just because we moved. It was going to be my senior year and I was fit to be tied. I was being put on the back burner and was doing a slow burn of my own. It just wasn't fair. My brother got to graduate with his friends. Why couldn't I? "Why?" I asked them. "Why do we have to move all the time?" Their response was a series of sighs and groans and "Here we go agains."

"Don't tell me," I said. "Let me guess. Status. It's status." It always came down to that.

"No Puerto Ricans here, boy," my father said.

"Or Gypsies," my mother said.

I told them their new middle class house was in the middle of the Mojave Desert. Here I was stuck light years away from civilization as I knew it. Life consisted of going from parking lot to parking lot. Not exactly a place to be without wheels. I'd have a marathon walk just to get a lousy pack of cigarettes. I had to leave my buddy Gypsy behind in our old neighborhood. It was the inner city but I missed the shit out of it. Going over to Gypsy's pad was nothing short of an expedition. If only Gypsy had his wheels already. He was expecting a hefty settlement from the paper factory where he got injured. Gypsy was a real-life Hungarian Gypsy with inky skin. Everybody called him Gypsy and the name stuck. He was slight, with small hands and delicate fingers, perfect for picking pockets. So said my racist family. It was a lot of bull. Gypsy only had half a thumb. The other half got cut off by a paper cutter where he worked since dropping out of high school. For a laugh, he'd stick his half-thumb into his ear and it would look like it was going right through his head, or he'd put his half-thumb by his groin to make it look like he was holding his dick. Once he pulled his stunt in a movie theater only to have this chick sitting next to him whack him in the nuts so hard he screamed like a freaking banshee. Man, I missed him.

The day before my first day at the new school, I was banging my soccer ball against the brick foundation of our new house when my old man whipped into our driveway. He braked so hard the old Chrysler rocked. The car had been in the shop for another brake job. My father had the brakes checked regularly to make sure no one was messing with them. Go figure. He was paranoid. About the Jews and the Rosenbergs and a secret society called the "*Nokmim.*" The unpronounceable Hebrew word meant "The Avengers." To me it sounded like something on the boob tube, but to my old man they were the ones who supposedly caught up with Adolf Eichmann, and, according to my father, they were bound to catch up with us and kill us all, one by one.

It was all a lot of bunk!

The car door slammed with a hollow, metallic bang. The door had been replaced when my father sideswiped a parked car a while ago. He was barely out of the old Chrysler, and he was already all over me. He said if I had to play sports I should play tennis, and not waste time on a back-alley game played by Gypsies and hooligans.

I ignored him. Using my left instep first, then my right, I kept kicking the ball against the brick foundation. My kicks were becoming harder and harder.

"Stop that. You want to cause damage, is that your new game?"

"That's it," I said in Hungarian. We spoke to each other in Hungarian as we always did.

"Every time you overdo it, your heart acts up. You're better off reading books."

The box my old man was trying to conceal under his arm looked too much like a book, a freaking medical book. He fished them out of the green garbage bin behind the hospital where he worked as a janitor. Before the Russians ruined my father's life, he had been a Royal Hungarian judge. Now he was a janitor and a royal pain in the ass. He told me he did not want me ending up like him. "A medical doctor was at all times and in all places immune to the whims of regimes," he said. The title of the last book was *Melanomas of the Breast*. It was filled with pictures of dissected breasts and words like "histology" and "fascia."

The box sat on the kitchen table when I came in. My father lit a cigarette from a new pack of Parliaments and watched me through the smoke. "Open it."

Instead of a book, the box contained my blue letter-sweater—minus the gold letter. He said he had the tailor remove it. The letter, he said, ruined an otherwise perfectly handsome sweater.

I told him I was never going to wear it and started to go up to my room. He followed. He said it looked stupid and American. Besides, how would it look, wearing my old colors in my new school? By the top of the stairs he was wheezing. I let him catch his breath so he wouldn't have one of his freaking asthma attacks. He explained in gasps that a big letter like that was unbecoming on a sweater, but if I wanted to I could hang it up on my wall. No, he hadn't thrown it out.

"I can't believe you did that," I said. "You have to ruin everything. It's just like the time my Aunt Piroshka sent me a soccer jersey from Budapest, and you wouldn't let me wear it because of that goddamm red star. Yeah, remember that? You made mother unstitch it." I yelled for my mother in the kitchen: "Tell him. Tell him."

My mother came out and said there was no reason for me to mouth off like that. She was a tiny woman but very strong, emotionally, physically, every which way. She was hard just like her granite features. I knew I was walking on thin ice. "Yes or no," I said. "Did you or did you not take off the red star from the soccer jersey your sister sent me? Remember? It was my Easter present."

She didn't remember. I did. Vividly. It was in 1953, the year Hungary beat England 7 to 1. I said to my father: "You came home drunk, remember?"

"Watch it, boy."

"You came home from your night watchman job and you wouldn't let me keep the soccer jersey because of the goddamm red star. You didn't care. That's what our World Cup team wore. You didn't give a crap how much it meant to me. All you cared about was your Persian rug with the swastika. Mother poured gallons of ink on it, remember? The freaking swastika bled through anyway. We almost got evicted, remember?"

My mother left and went upstairs. When she came back down with my sweater, my father was about to throw my ass out of the house. "You think I'm going to let you talk to me that way? I should've left you in Hungary. You would've made a great Communist."

"Heil Hitler," I gave my old man a Nazi salute.

He threw his cigarette pack in my face.

"Stop it, both of you," my mother said. She told my father not to work me up. She didn't feel like another trip to the doctor. Sometimes when I got overexcited I got breathless and my heart would act up. Our Hungarian doctor said I had an athletic heart.

My old man lit another cigarette with trembling fingers. After one drag, he grunted and put the cigarette out in his tea so it made a hissing sound. Then he left for the kitchen to take one of his pills. My mother tossed my letter sweater on the table. She had sewn the letter back.

I didn't acknowledge it.

"Look, son, your father is set in his ways. Sometimes he can be difficult to live with."

"I'm sure. I must've been difficult to live with, too, since you got rid of me."

"You're going to start all that again?" She looked hurt. "We were poor, son. You have no idea."

"Why didn't you send János?"

"You know why," she said. "You were your Aunt Piroshka's favorite. The poor woman couldn't have any children of her own. She had to have her womb taken out. Her first husband gave her syphilis. You're old enough to know what that means. She's lucky to have lived through it. She told me—I don't know if I ever told you this—that you're the only one who actually brought a ray of sunshine into her life." My mother was crying now. "Oh, son, you know how she doted on you."

"Doted? She was obsessed with me."

"You're going to sit here talking that way knowing she just passed? What kind of person are you?"

"What kind of person? What kind of person?? That's just it, Mother, I was never a person to her. And that goes for Uncle Arthúr, too."

My mother broke down now. She said, between sobs, I had no right to talk the way I did. I was too young to know what it was like under Communism.

I told her it must've been really bad for a mother to want to sell her son.

She got hysterical and demanded to know what in the name of Jesus I was talking about.

"Nothing," I said. "Just nothing."

She stopped crying and nodded her head slowly, took a deep breath with her eyes closed and nodded her head again. "Did you know how she died? Did you even bother to ask? She was found frozen to death in the Párisi Street apartment. In the foyer." My mother elaborated as if he had been an eye witness. "The poor woman probably fainted in the foyer. They found her blue. And you know what else? They had to pry a photograph from her hand. Guess whose picture it was? Yours! That's right. She had a death grip on your picture! God, it's awful." She took out a crumpled handkerchief and wiped her eyes.

My old man was still in the kitchen. I could hear him pacing. I lay down on the couch and started to flip through an old medical journal my old man brought home.

My mother left the room, I heard them mumble, then my father came back out. Good cop, bad cop. I didn't bother to look up.

He told me to sit up, and to put that magazine down. His wheezing simmered. I got up and turned on the television. The Warren Commission was coming close to releasing their report. *Insiders say the report is most likely to conclude that Lee Harvey Oswald was solely responsible for the killing of President Kennedy.* I waited for him to ask me to translate, to ask me who this Warren person was, but he didn't. I waited for him to wave his bony arms to indicate what he thought of the Warren Commission. That it was a cover-up, a burlesque. But he didn't do any of these things.

What he did was to turn off the television and in his calmest voice say, "Don't let your mother's histrionics fool you. Your aunt was killed. Some son of a bitch got to her. They're on to us. I'm telling you they're on to us. Jesus God. Your poor mother."

"What—are you talking about?"

"They're on to us."

"*They*? You're paranoid."

"Watch yourself."

"Well, you are."

"Is that all you have to say? Your Aunt Piroshka loved you like a son and that's all you have to say."

"The Hungarian secret police or whoever they are must have a lot of time on their hands to go after some old woman and to send agents all over the world for a dumpster diver."

"What d'you call me? What did you call your father, you hyena sucking son of a bitch?"

"Nothing," I said under my breath.

It was too late. What was said was said. I was ready to feel the stinging slap. My ear would smart, then ring. It shocked me my father didn't hit me.

I had gone too far. I said I was sorry.

"No you're not."

"It's just that you never listen. I tried to tell you the other day that Rosenberg was a common name."

He made an attempt to calm down. He waited. Followed his breathing. Sighed. Took a deep breath, let more air out. "Let me tell you something, son. It's not the name. I told you it wasn't the name. It's the face. I never forget a face. As a royal judge, I had to study faces. Different faces. The faces of criminals. I can tell you if a person's guilty by looking at his face. It's not just the look of guilt in the eyes, but the shape of the forehead. The closeness and position of the eyebrows. The hairline. There are three types of criminal countenances. One is the Neanderthal, another is the Negroid, and the third is the Ashkenazi Jew. Hooked nose, slumped shoulders, hairy back. That's where the Rosenbergs come in. You think I can forget a face? A resemblance to a face? As surely as I am standing here, I can see his father's face. Dangling from the gallows."

I turned to go. Out.

My old man reminded me that I couldn't run away from who I was. I couldn't run away from having been my aunt's *liebling*. "Come back here, you!"

Before I ran off, he wanted me to look at the instructions that came with his new medicine. It was supposed to make him breathe easier and to help with his mood and all that.

I dragged myself to the kitchen counter, where I found the old man's new medicine. Next to it was a printed piece of paper with the word WARNING large and bold. Patients taking this medicine, called an MAO Inhibitor, were to abstain from salami, red wine, ripe cheese, etc. All the foods my father ate all his life. Essentially it was my father's Hungarian diet.

He was standing right by me, his eyes magnified by his reading glasses. "Well, what?"

"Don't eat Hungarian, it says."

"Very funny." He snatched the paper from me and raised his voice. "Show me where it says Hungarian diet. I know that much English. Show me where it says that." The printed paper trembled in his hands. I went upstairs, taking my time. When I came down, it was with our bulky English-Hungarian Dictionary. I tossed it on the counter so it landed with a loud thud.

My old man had trouble breathing. He asked me just what the hell had gotten into me. I said I was going out.

"Go. But don't bring home any babies, you hear me?"

"God! I'm getting the hell out of here."

I slammed the door so hard the windows rattled. I heard the door open behind me. That's all I heard. The old man must have run out of air.

CHAPTER 2

For my first day of school, I took a long, steamy shower. For some weird reason I always had trouble tolerating a hot bath. I'd break out in hives and my heart would speed up like crazy, sometimes I couldn't catch my breath. After a sleepless night of tossing and turning and listening to the roar of jets as they took off and landed (That's another thing: our new house was close to Cleveland Hopkins Airport), I got up at the crack of dawn, scrubbed myself in the shower, put on a light blue dress shirt, gray trousers, and a brown sports coat. The final touch was a pair of black patent leather shoes with toes that came to a needle-point.

I rubbed some of my mother's VO5 hair cream into my scalp and slicked my hair back. At the kitchen table, I fished out a Camel from a fresh pack, lit it with my Zippo lighter, inhaled deeply, and let the air out through my nose. According to the kitchen clock, I still had a two-hour wait.

With its arched windows and ivy, Fairview High School could've been mistaken for a swank private college you see in movies. The school had its own football stadium and an indoor pool and all that. A humongous sign out front said the Fairview Warriors were state swimming champs for the last two seasons. I wasn't impressed.

And when I entered the halls of Fairview High for the first time as a senior transfer student, I knew why the school would never become an academic powerhouse. Girls. Girls. Girls. They were roaming the halls freely in tight sweaters and skirts that ended just above the knee. No uniform here like at my old all-boys school of ties and blazers, and grim religious retreats where the priests harangued you about masturbation. In homeroom, when everybody stood up to recite the Pledge of Allegiance, I almost freaking crossed myself. Old habits die hard.

The uproar in the halls seemed to continue right into my first period class. U.S. Government. I was early. Mostly empty seats. I took one in the middle of the room behind a yellow-haired girl. As the room filled up, I realized how out of place I was. All the suburban guys wore Madras shirts, white denims, and penny loafers without sox. They all had the same surfer haircut. Windblown and flyaway. Jesus. I should've skimped on the VO5 treatment. I might as well wear a button on my lapel that says *Greaser*. Should I hide my ballroom shoes under my seat? What kind of school was this anyhow? Where guys kept brushing their hair out of their eyes? Either they had blow dryers or they passed through a wind tunnel. Freaking surfers without a freaking ocean? I decided to relax and kick back. Let my shoes blind them. I tapped my pencil against the top of my desk in an absent-minded drum roll.

That's when she sat down at the empty desk next to mine. This real cute chick with shiny black hair and super blue eyes, and these long, curving lashes. Man! She smiled and said her name was Millie. I introduced myself with a stupid grin exposing my crooked teeth. I felt like an exchange student from Upper Slobovia. I said I was new. Millie nodded. She said she thought I was.

"Where you from?" she asked.

I told her I was from Hungary, that my family and I came here in '56.

"The Revolution, right? I remember seeing some stuff on TV. Did you have to escape?"

"Yup," I said casually.

Her eyes grew wide. "Wow," she said. "Bet that was scary."

"Ah, no big thing."

She said my English was real good. No accent. I told her I still had trouble pronouncing the *w* so it doesn't sound like a *v*. Like in "*v*ow." and "*v*erewolf."

She had a laugh at that. I could see a hint of pink bordering a super-even row of Chicklets teeth. Which made me feel a little uptight, not only because of my own teeth, but because this girl's interest in me was verging on the obvious.

Millie had very fair skin and this teeny-tiny nose. Unlike my hawk-like schnoz, hers was so, so delicate. Like porcelain from my aunt's china cabinet. It was the most beautiful nose I had ever seen.

She wore heavy black eyeliner that stretched beyond the corners of her blue eyes. It was sexy and scary. And kind of crazy. None of the other girls had make-up like that. Pretty frigging dramatic, man. Who did she think she was, Cleopatra? But the fact of the matter was, she was turning me on. Was that why she outlined her eyes? To turn guys on? What was she thinking? What was her mother thinking, letting her go out like that? What would my mother think if I brought a girl like that home? My mother would think her son hooked up with a whore. To my Hungarian mother, all American girls were whores. Too bad, I smiled to myself. That's what my mother gets for sending me to a school full of whores. Because, so far, I was enjoying myself.

A No.2 pencil rolled off Millie's desk. I picked it up and handed it to her. She had fine, small hands. That ready smile again, this time wider. Looks like Cleopatra was not afraid to show me her gummy smile. It was kind of weird. I kind of liked it.

On my long walk home after the first day of school, I felt pretty good about Fairview High. It was an unusually clear September day, and some leaves were already turning. A few yellow leaves were helicoptering onto the sidewalk in slow motion.

At supper, when my father asked me if they taught Latin at my new high school, I said, "Nope," and I said it as if I didn't give a crap. And I didn't. The only thing on my mind was this girl's smile.

The next morning I bumped into her in the hall outside our class. It was a warm and fuzzy feeling to know I would be bumping into her every day and sitting next to her for an entire year. Her hair and eyes were shiny and she had this fresh smell, not like perfume or anything like that, but the kind of smell that hits you when you open a Christmas present. She leaned against a locker in her pink pastel sweater telling me she lived only a few blocks from the school, off Bains Park. I no longer cared if my new high school was not an academic powerhouse. I found myself thriving on the general chaos in the hall and classroom. There was a short kid nicknamed Dwak, the class clown, who had our government class in an uproar. Dwak had a talent for making little saliva bubbles on the tip of his tongue and launching them among his classmates. Our government teacher proved to be powerless against Dwak, and a rowdy class hell-bent on senioritis. Mr. Powers had come out of retirement from a career as a trial lawyer only to be abused. His nickname was Flako because the skin on his face flaked. Mr. Powers hated to wear the button "Heads Up Football." How about, "Heads Up Government Study?" Now that got a laugh.

When I wasn't checking out Millie I was doodling my favorite cartoon character, Woody Woodpecker. Millie handed me a note asking if I would like to join the Art Club. She said she was the president. I was impressed but declined. I wrote back that I had zero talent as an artist. Woody Woodpecker was the only cartoon I could draw. I'd been practicing it like forever. Then I added a P.S.

The P.S. wanted to know if she liked football. My hand was sweating so much, the pencil was about to slide out of my frigging hand. Otherwise, I was in my cool mode.

"Yeah," she said.

I took it to be a definite "yeah."

Before the weekend, I dragged my mother to the Westgate Mall for a pair of loafers. I was sure to see Millie at the game.

She was a no-show. I spent the entire first quarter checking out the frigging bleachers. I went through a candy apple and half a pack of cigarettes. I was hoarse and pissed. Their kicker was no Pete Gogolak, that was for sure. I could've done better myself. By halftime I realized Millie wasn't coming and headed home. Like Mr. Powers, I didn't give a shit about football, either.

I was a little rattled in class Monday. Had half a mind to pay attention to Mr. Powers' nonsensical drone. After class Millie asked me if I went to the game. Yeah, I was there, no biggie. A week or so later I told her I was going to the school play, *Our Town*. Did she have any plans to go? Because if she did, I could meet her there.

A no-show. Again.

This time, she heard about it. I told her I was at the frigging play looking for her in the audience till I had a stiff neck. She said she was sorry she didn't go. She wasn't about to take a chance showing up by herself. What if I wasn't there? After all, it wasn't like an official date or anything.

I was freaked by official dates. My brother, who was two and a half years older, never went out on a date. It was such an American thing, corsages and all that. We had college and med school to worry about. We were told that getting serious before we had our M.D. in hand was not only stupid, but catastrophic. Our parents were doing everything in their power to make sure we got a college education, and I would have to do my part which included handing my paychecks from my part-time jobs over to my mother. Dating and anything resembling dating was out of the question. American girls, especially.

It looked like Millie was a lost cause. If I could just kiss her without all the fuss. As it turned out, I didn't have to ask her out. She asked me. The Friendship Formal was coming up, she said. It was tradition for girls who were in the Friendship Club to invite a guy to the dance. I was floored and had to muzzle my excitement. I scribbled a quick note back to her. Yes. But there was a problem with—ahem—my car, the GTO. It was impounded because of an unpaid speeding ticket.

"Oh nice," Millie said nervously, "I mean not so nice that it's in the pound." She asked when I'd get my car back.

"Next Saturday probably."

"How are you going to pick it up?"

"I was thinking of thumbing."

"I can drive you if you'd like."

"You drive?"

"I'll have to ask my mom for her car but she usually lets me borrow it."

"Great," I said.

I let my lie ride for a few days of chain-smoking tension. I was walking her home from school one cold afternoon when I let the cat out of the bag. I loved American cliches because for me it was usually the first time I heard them. It was so cold we could see our breath. Millie said my cold hands meant I had a warm heart. She gave me one of her mittens, so we could keep each other's hand warm. Now was the time to come clean. So—I didn't have a GTO after all. I didn't even have a car.

Millie reclaimed her hand. She looked bamboozled. "Why did you say you did?"

I felt stupid. Real stupid. "Just trying to impress I guess."

"You don't need to impress me, Art," she said.

"You still want to go out with me?"

"If you tell me how you escaped and all that, I might. You never told me how you got out of Hungary. What was it like?"

I told her how we were crammed together in a canvas-covered truck, heading toward the Austrian border in the middle of the night. "My father smeared black shoe polish on our faces so the Russians don't see us. It was a long ride to get to the border. You know where we had to go to the bathroom on the truck? In a hole in the floorboards. Thank God I didn't have to go. But I was sick to my stomach. I didn't know about the hole till our guide pointed his flashlight at it. He said, 'If you have to vomit, vomit through there.'"

"Were you scared?" Millie asked.

"No, just sick. I went to he back of the truck where there was an opening, like a flap. I thought if I got some air I wouldn't feel sick. That's when I saw these headlights gaining on us. We were being followed."

"Russians?"

"We didn't know. Nobody knew. Our guide thought it was the secret police. I thought I recognized the car. Because of the headlights. One was dimmer than the other. I was sure it was my uncle driving my mother and brother trying to catch up with us."

"What d'you mean your mother and brother? Didn't they escape with you?"

"No. My mother and father had a big fight before wc left. My mother didn't want to go. She was too scared, I guess. Anyway, the guide yelled for everybody to get down. He took out this big gun from under the hay. Everybody got down. Everybody except me. My father tried to pull me down but he wasn't quick enough. Then there was this loud flash. The gun went off. And I got hit."

"You were shot?!"

"Yeah. One of the bullets hit me. It was no big thing."

"What d'you mean no big thing?"

"No biggie. The bullet just grazed me. Lucky for me I had this ivory horn in my pocket."

"What were you doing with an ivory horn in your pocket?"

"My aunt gave it to me for good luck. I guess it was, because it took a bullet for me."

"You're not making this up."

"No, I'm not. It was blown to smithereens. All that's left is a chip. I'll have to show it to you sometime."

"How did you get shot again?"

"I was trying to stop the guide from shooting at my mother and brother. When the guide's gun went off, that's when I got hit. The truck braked like crazy. The guide got thrown off the truck. We all climbed out expecting the worst. That's when I knew for sure it was my uncle's car. My Uncle Arthúr's. It was steaming in the middle of the road with its hood bashed in. The headlights were still on. My uncle had run over our guide. It was a terrible accident. The truck driver got scared and took off without us. I looked for my mother and brother. They didn't come. My uncle couldn't get his car started. We had no other choice but to go on foot the rest of the way in a frozen canal so we wouldn't be seen. My hip felt alright where the bullet grazed me. Just a scratch or two. When my father poured some stuff on it, booze or something like that, that's when it stung. My freaking fingers were freezing. I had on all these layers of clothes my aunt gave me before we left. Even my gloves were from her. I remember working my fingers inside the gloves to keep warm. That's when this flare called Stalin's Torch went up. At first it looked like a shooting star. Then it was bright as daylight. We all hit the bottom of the canal."

"Oh my God." Millie said.

"I know. When I fell down, my knee crashed through the ice. There was nothing under it, only air. It was like glass breaking under my knee. Then came the afterglow. And the gunfire. The snow around me turned a freaky color of orange."

"Oh my God."

"It happened three more times. On No-Man's Land."

"No-Man's Land? What's No-Man's land?"

"It was like an empty field that belonged to nobody. Not to Hungary, not to Austria. We had to walk single file. I heard my father wheezing behind me. He had trouble catching his breath. Then out of nowhere a searchlight. Right in our faces. I was blinded like after a camera flash. Weird. Everybody froze. We thought we were caught for sure. I looked back to check on my father. He was lying on the ground."

This time Millie didn't say, "Oh my God." She just shook her head slowly. She couldn't believe it.

"The first thing I thought was maybe he got shot on the truck, too. It was pretty scary. My father would've died on the border if it wasn't for the Austrian Red Cross. The searchlight was from them looking for refugees. They were so efficient. They gave my father an oxygen mask and brought him back. He wasn't shot or anything like that. His asthma almost killed him, though. He only has one lung, the other lung was taken out."

"Did he have cancer?"

"No. Some sort of bad spot. Anyway, that's how it was explained to me."

"Okay. So, go on."

"Our rescuers spoke to us in German, one in broken Hungarian. They took care of the sick first, then the women and children. 'Women and children next. *Bitte Schön*.' It's German for please."

"Oh my God! Can I ask you something?" Millie asked sheepishly. "You have to promise you won't get mad."

"Okay."

"Were you really shot? Or did you make that up, too, just to impress me?"

"Yeah, I made up the whole Revolution. I'm a pathological liar."

"You are not. I wouldn't have invited you to the Friendship Formal if you were. Did you ever think about that?"

Millie arranged a double date so we had a ride to the dance. She even paid for the tickets in advance. All I would have to do was to rent a tux and buy her a corsage. It was set for Thanksgiving weekend. Plenty of time.

Plenty of time to kill myself, I thought. I was flat broke and had to bum a couple of bucks from Gypsy. A week or so before the dance, I told my parents I was going to another school play. A modern adaptation of a Shakespearean play where everybody was dressed in tuxedoes. But this time I was in it. Yup, I was in it. And my role required I wear a tuxedo. One which the school would provide. They were going to be surprised.

As a rule, my mother and father never attended any of my school functions, including my soccer games, thank the Lord, but on the appointed day they made an exception.

When I rushed into the house in my black tux and a white box containing the gardenia corsage, I freaked. My parents were all dressed to accompany me to the play. Even my brother János was there, dapper in suite and tie, glancing at his watch. My brother was a good-looking guy except for the unibrow and the hairy upper lip he had since the sixth grade when his nickname was Zorro. "Time to get going before the curtain goes up," he said. I had this feeling that he knew. I don't know how, but he knew.

"Oh, geez," I said to them. I was so sorry. I was totally uptight and it was no act. The frigging play was sold out. Why didn't they say anything? These Americans and their frigging school plays. They took them so seriously. We're going to look like a bunch of penguins. It was silly. "I'm really sorry. If only you would've said something. Geez."

I said I was supposed to be picked up at the end of the street. And I left.

The air was nice and cool. A nice evening for a stroll in a tux. I walked to the end of our street and kept on walking the ten blocks up 220th till I got to Cromwell, where Millie lived. Her street was lined on both sides with old buckeye trees.

The house was not brick, it was better than brick. It was a two-story frame house with a large bay window. A late model green Thunderbird and a Chevy convertible, top down, sat in the driveway. Both waxed and shined.

I rang the bell. Musical chimes. Her father opened the door. He was tall, very tall, blond and handsome. His hair was short-cropped. Razor cut. Probably a businessman and, unlike my father, probably successful. He was balancing a drink and a cigarette in one hand.

There was something wrong with his arm because he held it funny like it was frozen at an angle. "I'm Rhett," he said. "Rhett Weiler." I introduced myself using my Hungarian name. He did a quick take on me, then stepped back. An attractive redhead in a tight pink dress stood up holding a drink the same color as her husband's. She looked like one of Lawrence Welk's champagne ladies. She was Pat, Rhett said. Millie would be down shortly.

"I'm sorry. Would you say your Hungarian name again?" the mom asked.

I said my name again.

"Would you spell it?" She was slurring her words.

"A-t-t-i-l-a. I'm Attila Nagy. My father's name is Dr. Ferenc Nagy. But my American name is Art."

"Gotcha! Is your dad a doctor?"

"Juris Doctor," I said. I said it so fast it probably sounded like '*Jewish doctor.*'

There was no reaction. Lucky for me, Millie's folks were slow on the uptake.

They sat me down in front of a green marble fireplace, logs blazing. Rhett said, "Attila, huh? That's quite a name you were blessed with."

"There's an opera called *Attila* by Giuseppe Verdi," I offered in my defense.

"I didn't know that. Pat, did you know that?"

"No, I didn't."

Pat said, "We have a cleaning lady who comes now and then. Mrs. Grabowsky. She's Polish. Isn't she Polish, Rhett?"

"That she is."

"What kind of music do you like Mr. Weiler?" My attempt at small talk.

"American music."

Pat took a sip from her drink and smiled. "Can I have a cigarette, Rhett?"

Rhett got up and offered his pack of Chesterfields to Pat. She took one, Rhett reached into his pocket, produced a lighter and lit Pat's cigarette.

Pat smiled. Her teeth were not nearly as nice as Millie's. They were long and yellow. Otherwise, she was a pretty woman. A charm bracelet jingled from her wrist. She asked me how I liked Fairview High so far.

I said it was okay.

"I bet," Pat said. "Where did you say you went to school before Fairview High?"

"I went to Cathedral Latin."

"Oh brother, no kidding," Pat said. "That's where my brother Joe went. He ended up going to Notre Dame. I went to Rosemont College in Pennsylvania. With one of the Kennedy girls. Yup."

Rhett got up, looked up the mahogany staircase and said, "There she is."

Millie was coming down the staircase in a long baby-blue gown. It was strapless. She couldn't help but smile as she descended. When she got to the foot of the stairs, she swirled around like in a fashion show.

"Hold it," her father said. He was looking through the lens of his expensive-looking Kodak. "Stop."

Millie posed for the camera.

"Say cheez."

"Cheez," Millie said.

One flash. Then another.

"Dad, stop, please. I'm seeing spots. You want to blind me so I can't see my date."

Her Dad said she was already blind.

A laugh from Pat.

The quick jab wasn't lost on me. Nice shot. Looks like Mr. Rottweiler was a jealous dog.

"Okay, one more. For the album," Millie said.

"She's something in that outfit, isn't she?" her mother said.

I felt more comfortable on No-Man's Land, ducking Russian bullets. I should've spoken up, but didn't. I just stood there like an aardvark who wandered in from some bush country.

"Don't just stand there," Rhett said. "Move in closer. Put an arm around her, she won't bite."

Pat tilted her head back and blew smoke high in the air.

I was in awe of Millie. She looked different, older, more mature. Her shoulders, her back, and most of her chest were uncovered. Then these long white gloves reaching past her elbows. Whew! My hands were sweating. No wonder she wore gloves. Who would want to hold hands with a sweating animal? I was sweating, and not just my hands. And I was dying. Dying for a smoke.

When Rhett actually offered me a Chesterfield, because he did, I couldn't accept it. What would they think of a boy my age who smoked? "No, thank you," I said. I was polite in the extreme.

Our double date could not have shown up any sooner. My ass was baking. Either that or my tux was not such a good fit, after all. And there was nothing to do except stand there. An aardvark in a tuxedo.

I was still reeling from my meeting with the parents when I realized we were finally in the school gym and on the dance floor. Sweat was running down my back. The revolving crystal sphere hanging from the ceiling made me feel lightheaded. That, and holding Millie close to my body. I wondered if she could feel my heart banging against my ribs. She said they were playing her favorite song. *Blue Velvet.* I held her tight. Me and Millie were dancing slower than the rhythm of the Johnny Mathis number. My hand touched her bare back, and I felt something. Moles? She was not perfect. God, was I relieved!

I let my hand relax on her back.

"Ouch. Your cufflinks. Sometimes my moles bleed," she said.

I quickly removed my hand and put it back on her waist, where I could feel the material of her gown again. I felt awkward, but at the same time strangely *free*. That someone could talk to me about something so personal. Honestly like that. I looked around the gym, done in some New Orleans Mardi Gras theme, which to me didn't mean a whole lot. But then, in a way, it did. There were other worlds out there, and the one that came with Millie Weiler was turning out to be—pretty freaking far out. I felt like I wandered onto an exotic movie set where just about anything could happen. It looked like I was already part of the cast. Kids in fancy-ass tuxedoes. Couples in fairy tale costumes dancing their butts off on a basketball court. A princess wearing long white gloves offered me her arm.

A few cupfuls of the spiked punch and I lost it. Came up with something really stupid. I was trying to be, I don't know, like romantic. I told Millie how the crystal sphere made her back look real neat with all sorts of colored…spots. Jesus! Did I actually say *spots*? With all the moles on her back? Nice going, jerk off!

"Oh God," she said. Then she laughed. She laughed so hard her breasts shook in her strapless formal. Nice. I wasn't sure what any of this meant. But I was sure of one thing. I wanted to see this girl again. And not only on school days. I really wanted to get to know her.

We had already made plans to work on a government class project the next day, a Sunday. The first real snowfall. Her parents were out Christmas shopping leaving the two of us alone. Our project had to do with the assassination of President Kennedy and the Warren Commission. Millie asked where I was when Kennedy was shot. I told her I was on a bus with my grandmother, who was visiting from Hungary at the time. I had taken her to Sears to get her some comfortable tennis shoes, and she picked out a pair of black ankle-length Keds she wore home on the bus. She was a tiny woman and her feet didn't reach the floor. Someone had a transistor radio. "That's how we found out Kennedy was shot. I translated it for my grandmother, and she started crying. She fished out her rosary and said the rosary right there on the bus. I wasn't embarrassed or anything. I was too freaked about the shooting. When we got off, I called my mother from a pay phone. I must've been breathless because my mother told me to slow down and follow my breathing. Her reaction sort of shocked me. She said maybe the next President won't handle the Russians with kid gloves."

"She actually said that?"

"Weird or what? What about you, Millie? What were you doing when Kennedy was shot?"

"I was in my typing class. All of a sudden kids were running up and down the hall shouting, 'Kennedy's been shot. Kennedy's been shot.' My parents were pretty upset. I mean they weren't crying or anything. Just upset. But later—it may have been the next day, I don't know—when they showed Ruby being escorted by these guys in cowboy hats, my mom said, 'Oboy. Bet you something's going to happen. I can feel it.' And bam. Right on TV. Ruby shoots Oswald."

"I know," I said. "I saw the same thing with my grandmother. She couldn't believe it. 'What kind of country is this?' she said."

"Geez," Millie said.

I told Millie my father thought Kennedy was killed by the government. The CIA, to be exact. He said they were American patriots who refused to watch their country bend over for the Russians.

Millie raised her right eyebrow. "Maybe we should put that into our report for class."

"You're kidding, right?"

"What d'you think?"

In terms of any real work on our project, very little got done. Our books were left open on the dining room table. We sat there talking about everything except government. Millie told me her Dad was weird, too. He was a tyrant. Sometimes he was downright mean. "One time," she said, "when I was around four my Dad came down to the basement and saw I had my toys all over the place. He was so mad he made me get into this cedar chest where I should've put the toys. Then he sat on it so I couldn't get out. He thought I'd scream and panic, and he'd teach me a lesson. Somehow I knew if I reacted he'd get worse, so I just played dead. After a while, my Dad got bored and let me out."

"Nice," I said.

"Do you get along with your Dad?"

"Yeah."

"Is there anybody you don't get along with."

"I get along with everybody. Except my brother. I'd like to kill him."

She laughed.

"This one time we were playing swords. We were just kids. I was almost nine. I was spending the summer in my mother's hick town for a change. My brother is two and a half years older and he knows it. Anyway, we're getting ready to play swords, right? Somehow his sword was always longer. And sharper. Before I knew it, he was making a spear. My father told us never to sharpen the sticks because we could gouge out each other's eyes. You'd think my brother listened? I'd say, 'Remember what father said.' He plain ignored me. There he'd be, crouched down at the foot of the acacia tree sharpening his spear to a pencil point. He kept taunting me by saying I was scared to go to America."

"Were you?" Millie asked.

"I was. But I didn't like being teased about it. He was a real ass. He'd say, 'They've got guns there and Indians and cowboys and you're scared.' To tell you the truth, I wasn't scared so much of going as of leaving. I don't know. I couldn't explain if I wanted to."

For a long time we didn't say anything, just stared at each other. I stood by the door ready to go when I looked at Millie. I mean, really looked at her. It was not her black sweater and plaid skirt or black pumps. It was her eyes. They were taking me in. I told her she was beautiful. I was looking at her lips. Their texture reminded me of soft poppies. Millie was waiting for me to kiss her. I kissed her gently on the mouth. Her lips were soft. I felt electricity. I kissed her again, harder.

As I walked home, the feeling stayed with me. Her smell, the way her lips felt, the softness, her scented hair. The warmth of her body. The kiss kept replaying itself over and over in my head. I felt happy. For no special reason. Could one kiss do all that?

What was happening to me? Something was, that's for sure. It took me no time at all to get to my new brick house. Even in the snow, the walk wasn't so far after all. My heart was beating fast, and I was happy about that, too. I had all this energy out of nowhere, and once I got home, I decided to shovel our walk and driveway. I was half done when my father came out in his long winter coat. He looked surprised. Shocked, would be a better word. He gave me his gloves. We shared a cigarette. He said I shouldn't be smoking. I said I knew.

"So what's up? It's unlike you to be helping your old man with the snow."

We had a laugh.

"By the way," my father said, "what character did you play in that fancy tuxedo, Hamlet?"

"How d'you know?"

"Just a guess."

CHAPTER 3

We were snowed in for most of our Christmas break. Close to 12 inches. It didn't stop me from going over to see Millie. Once the two of us even made it to the shopping center and Stouffer's, for their famous hot fudge sundae with the cherry on top. Another nice thing about America was that we could have freaking ice cream in the winter without worrying about getting sick. Hungarians had pretty set ideas about health, I was telling Millie. Like being out in the cold could give you a cold. My old man was a walking laundry list of medical warnings. Smoking was okay but A/C could lead to pneumonia. A draft which to most Americans meant a nice cool breeze was very close to being lethal. It could lead to sinusitis, influenza, pleurisy, pneumonia, coma, and death. We knew of a Hungarian family who drove through the entire state of Florida with the windows up, scared to death of a little breeze.

"I'd die," Millie said. "How 'bout a convertible? What would they say about that?"

"Death carriage."

"Oh geez."

I told her it wasn't a rollover they were afraid of, but the draft. Everything boiled down to that freaking draft! And drinking and exercise. "When I say drinking I mean water. My father said it could lead to pneumothorax, some horrible crap like that. Oh yeah, that's when your lung collapsed from shock, I think the old man said. I almost collapsed alright, right after a soccer game, and it wasn't from drinking any water. It was from *not* drinking water. I was freaking dehydrated."

Millie took me by a men's store and had me wait outside so I wouldn't spoil her surprise. She was going to get me something for Christmas. When she came out, the present was already gift-wrapped. She wouldn't give me any clues except that it was something I could use. Something to keep me warm.

"A hat?"

"No."

"Gloves?"

"Nope."

"Hand warmer?"

She shook her head, put her mitten to my mouth. "Stop it, for Pete's sake. Stop guessing. I'm not going to tell you."

OK. I was pretty sure she got me gloves. My hands were always cold. I was warming up to the idea of getting a pair of nice gloves for Christmas, when she said: "You know what? I might as well give it to you now. It's freezing out. We got a ways to go yet."

She was right. The wind was really something else. Besides, it wasn't like we'd get to open our presents together under the old tree or anything. A couple of days ago, I showed up at her house early, and her Dad came to the door, saying they were eating dinner. Then he closed the door on my face. I never told Millie. Being together for Christmas at my house wasn't going to happen, either.

"Well, are you going to open it?"

I hesitated. It was wrapped so nicely. We stopped under a light of swirling snow. I put the ribbon and fancy paper into my pocket. Too bad I would have no one to show how nice it was wrapped. I never got anything wrapped like that. Now, let's see. What is in the box? I opened it. They were ear muffs. Fuzzy and fluorescent green. Yeaow!

"You don't like them," she said.

"No, I do."

"Well, put them on."

I put them on and looked at her. I felt like a dog wearing a hat.

"Now I know you don't like them."

I told her it wasn't that. Actually it *was* that. I thought they were dumb as shit. I knew other guys were wearing them and all that, but…me? I really needed to accentuate my ears. She said she thought the color green was nice and Christmasy. I told her she was right about that. With my green ears and red nose I felt like a Christmas elf.

She gave me the receipt and said I could take it back and get something else.

I did. The next day, on Christmas Eve, I sloshed back in the snow and got me a pair of gloves, and for Millie a 45 LP of "Ticket to Ride" by the Beatles. I called her from a frosty phone booth and told her what I got. She thanked me for my gift. I told her I wanted to take it over but they would probably be eating. With Christmas Eve and all that. She was sorry we couldn't get together. She said they would open their presents early the next morning. I thought that was pretty dumb and said so. She said she thought it was dumb we opened ours Christmas Eve. I told her how commercial Christmas was in America. Presents. Presents. Presents. Taking Christ out of *Christ*mas. What about the freaking Holy Family? I told her what I thought of their artificial tree. Millie and me kinda got into it, then let it drop.

On the way home both my ears and hands were cold. The gloves were some synthetic shit that made it worse. It acted like some kind of freaking conductor.

By the time I got home, my fingers were numb. All the lights were off in the house except for the Christmas tree in the living room. There was no car in the driveway, which meant only my brother was home. When I opened the door, I overheard my brother singing "Silent Night" in German. *Shtille Nacht. Heilige Nacht.* He didn't know I was there. He was sitting under our lit tree singing like some freaking little drummer boy. I was afraid to let him know I heard him because he'd beat the crap out of me. I tip-toed back out and came back in with a bang of the door and a cough so he could recover himself.

Later that night, we opened our Christmas presents. My brother got me a pair of gloves, as did my uncle. The same, cheap, synthetic shit I got for myself. Now I had three pairs. My father got the real toy, a Webcor tape recorder that cost a fortune. It was a present for the family, I was told. Of course I was not allowed to go near it. They said everything I touched turned to crap. My father had pre-recorded a Christmas message meant to be heard by our guests, who arrived barely an hour after we opened our presents. Our Christmas guests were Uncle Arthúr and Endre Szabó, a self-proclaimed art connoisseur and an avowed alcoholic, who showed up with Anna, of all people. It seemed my uncle and Anna had a falling out.

My father's taped Christmas message promised a bright future without the specter of Communism and a return to our homeland as a return to Canaan. But it would not be without cost. It would take war. Yes, war, my father warned on the tape. He was making dangerous predictions for the new year and for the coming years. You could hear him cough on the tape as he cleared his one lung: "Nasser is on his way up. Watch his star."

While the tape was running, Endre Szabó whispered that he had to leave for an hour or so, but he'd be back.

My father enjoyed listening to the sound of his voice, especially after a glass of wine or three. There was a reckless cynicism in his voice. "Keep an eye on good old Nasser. He's a little Hitler, you know." It might sound like blasphemy to some ears in America, he said, but it was true. Little Hitler was rising in the east. Once he played out his dire prediction, he had my brother stop the tape. "And now," my father said, raising his glass, "I'd like to offer a toast to Dr. Arthúr Kun. Take the floor, if you please, Dr. Kun."

My uncle and old man both had doctorates in Jurisprudence. Now and then they'd refer to each other as doctor. In America it was meaningless, like being a count of no account. My brother pushed the "record" button. My uncle tried waving my father off, but it was only a token gesture. We all knew he had a mouthful to say. His first allusion was sexual, then he turned to politics. "The United States and the Russians are in it together," he said.

"Hold the mike closer," my father said in a tired voice. He didn't really want to hear this. He had to squint to concentrate. Once my old man had his say—and on tape—that was it.

He tapped his shirt pocket for a cigarette. He was out. He signaled to me to get him a fresh pack from the kitchen. Only one pack was left in the drawer. I opened it, took a few out for myself, and jiggled the pack so he wouldn't miss them. I pulled two forward and offered my father a cigarette. He thanked me. Anna came in from the bathroom which opened right off the dining room. She had just flushed the toilet. My uncle said, "Ahh, there's nothing lovelier than the stink of shit." I knew my uncle didn't intend to be vulgar. It was just the way he talked. His way of saying that the house his sister-in-law's family jumped into buying was weirdly constructed, and this was how he let them know. How could the room where people shitted open from the room people ate in? Sometimes I wondered how my uncle was able to get a university degree with a mouth like that.

"You're a pig. I swear to God you're a pig," my mother said.

"So I'm a pig," my uncle said. He held up his glass. It was not a toast, he was out of wine.

"You had enough," my mother said.

Anna was crying into her hand. She probably wished Endre would've stayed with her instead of going to his goddamm AA meeting.

"Come here, baby," my Uncle Arthúr said to Anna. "Someone bring baby to me."

My mother went over and whispered into Anna's ear.

My father lit up another of his Parliaments and watched through the smoke.

Reluctantly, Anna went over to where my uncle was sitting. She looked like she wasn't going to humor him, not this time.

Uncle Arthúr pulled her onto his lap. His tongue was out half way and to the side. It was the look of concentration, as if he was doing a difficult task. Then he winked around the room and started to give Anna a little horsy ride.

"This is lovely," my father said.

I was sure glad Millie wasn't here. Jesus! Could it get any worse. It did.

Anna blanched, turned color. She took the mike and whacked my uncle on the side of the head. He released her instantly.

"Bravo," my father said. My father was a gentleman who in public always sided with women, but in private few women trusted his phony chivalry. The "Bravo" fell flat. And Anna was already kissing my uncle on the spot where the mike broke the skin. She was sorry. Baby was sorry. She was going to make it better, and everybody was probably thinking, oh my God, how nice. The two were making up. As Anna got off his lap she received an affectionate tap on the fanny.

Uncle Arthúr was well on his way. "…So that anyone who thinks the world is heading back to its old ways is mistaken. I predict that in ten years we're going to find that nothing has changed. So—Stalin's body is out on the street. But there is no sign of Chinese militarism gathering strength. The Soviets and the United States will continue to keep western Europe and the Chinese out in the cold. As for your Nasser, he is insignificant. A pawn. The Jews in Tel Aviv don't matter. It's the Jews in New York. The bankers. Who do you think owns this house? You? Hahah! Keep sending your payments to New Jersey and pretend it's not Jew York. Go ahead. Be my guest."

"Christ was a Jew," I said.

They all looked at me like I committed a foul or something. My father said, "Can't you shut the hell up? It's Christmas Eve for Chrissake!?

"That's the point. He was born a Jew," I said.

"But he was baptized," my mother said.

"Here we go again," my uncle said.

My father coughed, this time loud enough for the running tape to record his cough. It was the cough of dissent. And the cough of dissent was for the record. Portions of the tape would have to be erased, I heard my father mumble under his breath.

"I submit," my father said, "that in a year or two's time we'll have war. Yes, war." He looked around the room for a reaction. I knew my father, he wanted to be shocking. And it was going to start with that little Hitler from the East. "Give Nasser a year or two but watch his star! And I wouldn't give up on Christianity so easily, my friend," my father said with forced eloquence.

Uncle Arthúr smiled. All of my father's predictions had been wrong over the years.

"I am first a Christian, then a Hungarian!" my father said. "And that's how I'm raising my boys." He looked toward me and my brother. I didn't know about my brother but I had pretty good eye contact with my shoes.

"Then they're in trouble," I heard my uncle reply. I looked up. My uncle stabbed his own chest with his thumb: "I'm a man first and foremost." He punctuated his last sentence by weighing his balls.

There was a loud knocking on the door.

We looked at one another without saying a word. It was so quiet we could hear the silk sound of the running tape.

The door opened.

It was Endre Szabó. He was shit-faced drunk. "Merry fucking Christmas."

For the next several days through Christmas break, I showed up like clockwork at Millie's back porch. And once we were back at school, I walked Millie to her classes, had lunch with her, walked her home, and we worked on homework together until dinner. Then we'd yak on the phone till late at night. Millie told me she'd like to go out now and then. "You know, out?" She said her Dad hated guys who slinked around the back door. He liked wholesome American guys who were at least as tall as he was, which was six-four, and had some moolah. He had trouble coping with the fact that I wasn't over six feet and I appeared cheap since I didn't even take her to a movie. She said he would tease her mercilessly about me not being what her Dad called "Your common variety American hunk." He would even say sarcastic things like, "Nice catch, Millie!" He commented about the way I dressed. I wore the same letter sweater from my old school, day after day like a uniform.

No, I'd never be the "helluva guy" Millie's parents expected, but to Millie I was perfect the way I was. Hey, they could shove it. Shove it, Rhett. Shove it, Pat.

Millie made no bones about saying what she thought of her Dad when he talked shit about me. So what if I was the back door type? So what? It didn't seem to bother Millie in the least that I didn't drive. So what if it pissed off her Dad I didn't have a driver's license?

One evening, we were watching TV together when Millie's Dad went on the attack and Millie stood up for me.

"Art's a Hungarian refugee, Dad," Millie told her father when he got nasty about me not having a car.

Her Dad glanced up from his paper, bored. "Is he a citizen?"

"He is. Aren't you, Art?"

"I am, Mr. Weiler."

Her Dad continued talking like I wasn't in the room. "Then why didn't he change his name?"

That one stung.

Once we were alone, Millie told me she felt bad about the way her Dad was treating me. If I never showed up again, she said, she wouldn't blame me. Most guys didn't. The only guys who ever showed up for a second date with her were these basketball player types, she said, and she'd get a stiff neck dancing with them. All they wanted to talk about was surfing. She let me know she didn't care for guys who followed every wave in the fad-world. She said she admired the way I held my ground. My refusal to look like I was "with it" was almost heroic. And this included my ballroom shoes. Millie told me she really appreciated how I went out of my way to be extra nice to her artsy-fartsy friends—and to her Dad. She said it showed I had a good heart. That bugged her Dad the most, Millie said. That and the fact that I kept showing up at their back door.

I once tried telling Millie's father how lucky they were here in America. I told him a lot of people in Eastern Europe didn't eat as well as their collie, Bonnie. It was meant as a compliment.

"Huh." Mr. Weiler's response was more of a grunt than a word. Mr. Weiler cocked his head in the direction of Bonnie, who was lapping up her Purina Dog Chow. "We have more if you want it," he said.

"What Art meant was—"

"I know what he meant."

"You're being mean, Dad."

Millie told her father we were going out.

"In the rain, for Chrissake?"

"Mom said I could use her car so we could see James Mason in *The Desert Fox*, then go out for pizza."

Her Dad grunted again.

To soften him Millie said she told me about Uncle Larry. How Uncle Larry, her Dad's brother, died in World War II. Shot down during a bombing run over Italy. She mentioned Uncle Larry's Purple Heart.

"Alright already," Mr. Weiler said. "Go."

Then he glared at Millie's skirt. The glare meant it was too short. His open palms made a lowering motion. But that wasn't enough. He had to add a little jab. "Not wearing heels tonight I see."

The bad news was Mr. Weiler was turning out to be quite the asshole. The good news was Millie was of the same opinion.

We didn't see James Mason in the *The Desert Fox* that night. We kissed as soon as we were alone in her mother's car. The rain stopped. She put the convertible top down at the first red light and turned the heat up full blast. Millie had something for me. A wallet-size of her senior picture showing her shiny black hair flipped up by her shoulders. She said it was called a Jackie Kennedy. She wore a dark sweater and pearls around her neck. I thanked her and said it was beautiful.

"Turn it over," she said.

On the back of her picture she wrote:

> *Less than the cloud to the wind*
> *Less than the foam to the sea*
> *I am to thee*

I thanked her and gave her a kiss at the next red light. Millie made a turn and parked. She got out of the car and opened the passenger side. I scooted over behind the wheel. I put the car in gear and drove off.

I already saw the movie *The Desert Fox* with my father so I told Millie all about it once we were on our way. This was not my first driving lesson. Millie had been secretly teaching me every time we were supposed to go to the movies. I told Millie my father cried like a baby when he saw Rommel and his Germans losing. The Hungarians were on the German side during the war, I said. They lost a great battle by the Don River somewhere in Russia. "My Uncle Arthúr was there. Unlike your uncle who got a Purple Heart, all mine got was five years in a Gulag for being on the wrong side. Anyways, I found myself rooting for the Allies in the movie. My father didn't like that. He didn't like that at all."

Millie scrunched up her face: "Is your dad a Nazi?"

"No, he's crazy. Like me. My old man's okay. He's just a little paranoid about a couple of things." I gave Millie a run-down of my father's dislikes. Not the complete list, more like a small sampling. "My father's paranoid about Communists, just like that McCarthy guy we heard about in class. He also doesn't like me eating buttered popcorn in the movie theater. Any Hungarian worth his salt would never butter his popcorn. It just isn't done. It's as unnatural as putting cherries on your ice cream. Chocolate syrup was okay or hot fudge, but cherries no. Fruit and milk didn't mix unless you wanted them to curdle in your stomach. Hungarians and Americans didn't mix either, unless you were bent on diluting your blood.

"Your dad sounds like a real lulu," Millie said.

"Yeah, he's funny. Not ha-ha funny, just crazy funny. I think I told you he was a judge back home, then a night watchman in a cherry orchard, right? And now he works as a janitor at Fairview Hospital. Well, to get a rise out of him I once had him paged at the hospital: *Calling Dr. Ferenc Nagy. Calling Dr. Rosenberg. Drs. Nagy and Rosenberg to Surgery. We have a Code Blue in surgery.*"

"You didn't. You're terrible," Millie said.

"I had to. He's paranoid."

Millie found herself laughing so hard I could see her gums. She was wiping the tears from her eyes with Kleenex.

"Who's Dr. Rosenberg?" she asked.

"I dunno. I think his first name is Julius."

"Yeah. And his wife's name is Ethel. You're one crazy maniac, you know that? Can you be serious for just one minute? Am I ever going to meet your father?"

Not if I can help it, I thought. I was scared shitless introducing Millie to my father the judge. I told her he would most likely interrogate her about her lack of knowledge of classical music. If Millie didn't know who Ludwig van Beethoven was, she didn't stand a chance. She might as well pack it in.

"*Roll over Beethoven*," Millie sang as I barreled down the Valley in her mom's Chevy convertible.

I drummed a four-one beat on the dash.

"*Roll over Beethoven*."

I was going nutso on the dash.

"Hey, buddy, keep your hands on the steering wheel."

The drive down the Valley was pretty steep. I coasted down the incline and pumped on the brakes like Millie taught me. I was driving with one hand, my elbow dangling out the window. It was pretty nippy outside, but we had the heat on full blast. The wind was blowing our hair every which way. We really dug it. It was great in America where you could waste heat on the open air. And this girl Millie seemed to like the way we were rocking and rolling in the Chevy convertible—and without the radio on. She said I was better than a radio. When I wasn't playing drums on the dash I'd be playing with her. I'd take the wheel in one hand and massage her thigh with the other. Then my hand would start inching up. I was touching the soft band of skin between hose and girdle when she stopped me.

She said I better slow down. We'd better slow down.

"Oh-kay," I said.

After an awkward silence I asked Millie out for an "official" date. I knew she loved to skate. I offered to take her to an open air rink called Winterhurst. My soccer buddy Gypsy would pick us up. He finally got his wheels, a spiffy fire-engine red Mustang Fastback. I told Millie how Gypsy lost half his thumb for it.

She was horrified: "Yikes, the poor guy."

Somehow I (we) lost momentum. I didn't make it past the kissing stage that evening. After pizza at Shakeys we headed toward my house. I was still doing the driving. I stopped the car a safe block away from my street. I told Millie my parents would be spooked seeing me behind the wheel without a learner's permit.

"I'd say you're learning pretty fast," Millie said. As she said this she patted my thigh.

When she drove off, I realized I didn't kiss her goodnight. I gave her a half hour to get home before I called her to tell her I missed her. My brother overheard and shook his head. Once I was off the phone, I mustered up enough courage to show János Millie's picture.

"Aha," my brother said.

I forgot about the little poem on the back and was immediately sorry for sharing.

"The poem is plagiarized," my brother said.

"No it's not."

"Oh yeah? Who uses words like *thee*? Huh?"

"It's poetic," I said.

"It's not poetic. It's pathetic."

"Give me back the picture."

My brother tossed it back at me.

"Hey, watch that."

"*Hey, watch that*," my brother mimicked.

Me and Gypsy picked up Millie in the Fastback. With his driving gloves and cap Millie's mom said he looked like he was heading to the Grand Prix instead of a skating rink. Once we got in, Gypsy floored it. He shifted, double clutched, and really opened her up on curving Rocky River Drive, blowing off five cars at a time. Millie was petrified, her head glued against the headrest. I held on in the back seat, my cigarette remaining unlit between my shaky fingers. I hoped I'd live long enough to get to skate with my date. "What d'you think?" I shouted to Millie over the whine of the engine. "Fast," she squealed.

Gypsy laughed like a maniac, downshifted and made another of his daring cuts, right in front of a CTS bus.

The Fastback got us to Winterhurst in record time.

Only Millie had skates. Light blue figure skates with rabbit fur trim and pom-poms. Silver blade with serrated tip.

I rented a pair of brown hockey skates and was eager to test them on the ice. The truth of it was I didn't want Millie to see my shoe size. A large red number 8 was sewn on the heels. Now everyone could see that Attila the Hun was a closet twinkle toes. Unlike these larger than life American hockey stars zooming past me with sizes like 11 and 12. What did these people eat?!

I left Millie sitting on the bench, lacing up her skates. Crap. I should be giving her a hand instead of feeling sorry for myself. I went back to her. I made up to her by dropping on my knees in front of her, as if I was asking for her hand. "Can I help?"

"I'll let you," she said and smiled.

My face was inches from her black leotards. Her light blue skates tapered up nicely to her smooth calves. I wondered if she noticed my shoe size.

"What's your shoe size?" I asked Millie.

"Same as yours," she said.

My first thought was that I should've asked for at least a 9 and put up with the wobbling and the pain.

"I have big feet," she said.

"No you don't."

Gypsy came by and said he was going home.

"What?"

He said he had a pair of skates rusting in his basement, if he could find them. I offered to rent him a pair. "Naw," Gypsy passed. I wondered what his shoe size was. A six? "It had to be the right fit. He was pretty spastic on the ice," he said. Before leaving, Gypsy bought a hot chocolate for each of us.

I was still on my knees, tightening Millie's light blue figure skates when she said Gypsy seemed like a nice guy. "Why do you call him Gypsy?"

"Because he is," I said. "He's a Hungarian Gypsy." I told her Gypsies were originally from India. That's why they had that inky-colored skin. The trouble was most Hungarians hated them. It was a racist thing. Like Blacks in America.

"I'm glad you're not a racist."

"I don't know," I said. I looked up at Millie. She was playing with a loose strand in her hair. In her black leotards and angora turtleneck, and with her hair swept up, she looked like a goddamm music box dancer. "God, you're beautiful," I said.

"Stop it," she said. "You're embarrassing me. Are you Hungarians always so fast?"

"Always," I said.

I held her while she took baby steps to get to the white glow of the rink.

"Couples only," the disc jockey announced. The first score was "Jingle Bell Rock." I took Millie's gloved hands and it surprised me again and again how small they were. We glided off. The colored lights moving around the ice reminded me of the crystal sphere at the Friendship Formal. This was more my territory, since it was closer to the old neighborhood. I was a pretty fair skater, Millie was excellent. She was telling me about the artificial plastic pond in her back yard where her Dad ran the hose and the puddle froze over. That's where she practiced. It was great, she said.

We were off again. Cutting through the cool air in tandem. It was like flying, like going up in the air for a bicycle kick, except here the bicycle was built for two. It was not about scoring or not scoring, but like being in sync.

Millie loved skating. The excitement and the cool air reddened her cheeks. We skated the next number and the one after that.

> Olah-etta olah-etta
> In the Jungle the mighty jungle
> The lion sleeps tonight

I pulled her closer. We leaned into the air together, our skates gliding in long, smooth sweeps.

The pace speeded up. The next number was some unfamiliar tune from Russia of all places. It wasn't "Midnight in Moscow" but something really fast. We could barely keep up. No, we couldn't keep up. We noticed some guy in the center of the rink, dressed like some kind of Olympic ice skater. A billowing shirt and these black super-tight bell-bottoms, and he was in the middle of a spin. Only when he stopped did we realize it was Gypsy, for Chrissake.

Gypsy!

We had to lean on each other we were laughing so hard. He was something, this Gypsy. Before long everyone was watching. Gypsy was a real wizard on the ice. 'Course I knew. Gypsy and me set the whole thing up. The disc jockey, a friend of Gypsy's, was in on it, too. Gypsy was now doing a Russian dance. He looked like he was squatting, arms locked in front of his chest. Then he alternated kicking his legs out from under him to the frenetic pace of *Kalinka*. That's what the disc jockey called this cool Russian number. Everyone on the ice clapped their hands to keep time.

Millie was clapping her hands and laughing. This was great, she said. Just great. She had her gloves off now, and so did I. I took her hand and held it. There was that electricity again. The same electricity as when I kissed her for the first time.

She had very white, very soft hands. Slim fingers. Lilac nail-beds. I took her hand and held it and said nothing. We watched these huge snowflakes fall and melt on the ice. We kept holding hands except when we patted Gypsy on the back for his "grand" performance. We held hands during the next number, "Blue Hawaii."

"Couples Only."

On our next date, I took Millie on a night sled ride down the Valley. I knew of a pretty secluded (and steep) course that snaked down among the trees. Gypsy dropped us off again but this time my brother János was supposed to pick us up. I had a pretty short sled, and the only way it could fit two was if we lay on top of each other.

Which was exactly how we went down the hill. We took turns. Sometimes I was on top while Millie steered. Then we switched. Either way, it felt just great. It looked like Millie was digging it, too. Steering was next to impossible, but we didn't care as long as we avoided the trees. Most of the time we flipped over, sometimes on purpose so we could roll into the snow and I could fall on top of her and kiss her. Once as we rolled into each other in the snow, we stopped laughing. I ended up on top of her, breathing hard. I kissed her with my tongue. Like I was hungry for her.

There was no one else at the bottom of the hill. The stars were out. Zillions of them. I put my arm around Millie. I showed her the Big Dipper and the Little Dipper, and farther off, a star that was so bright, it was called a Diamond Star of the 4th Magnitude or something crazy like that. Then a shooting star. "There," I said. "Up there!"

"Wow." She said she loved to look at the stars but never knew the constellations.

It was cold and getting late, and we snuggled some more, doing just fine keeping each other warm. I eventually built a small fire to warm our hands. "Millie. *Millie*," I said, "Is that your full name? I mean, is that what it says on your birth certificate?"

She said it was short for Lyudmilla.

"Russian? You're kidding."

"Now, why would I be kidding, you silly."

I was a bit fazed. "Why would your all-American parents give you a Russian name?"

"My mom liked it, I guess. She went to some fancy school up east. I'm sure you heard about it. With one of the Kennedy girls. Anyway, they were reading this long Russian poem, *Ruslan and Lyudmilla*, I think by Pushkin. She just liked the name. I like the name, too. It's kind of different and neat, don't you think? My Dad thinks my mom is part Russian. You know, way back."

"It's some name," I said. I told her I may be able to recall a few lines of the Pushkin poem. "Believe it or not, in Hungary we had to learn Russian and memorize parts of it. Then translate it into Hungarian. My English may be pretty rough. Let's see:

> *Behold a shiny warrior on his horse*
> *Armed with tongues of flame,*
> *Born of thunder and the stars,*
> *See how he holds its shaggy mane,*
> *How he blows the poet's horn.*

Instead of being awed, she said, "You shit." That's the first time I heard her use language like that. But it was affectionate-like. "You!" she said. "You liar. You memorized it in that Marionist school of yours. Giving me that stuff about translating it and all that. Give me a break."

"You know what my last name, Nagy, means in English? 'Great.' It means 'Great.' Technically, my full name is Attila the Great."

"You're full of it," she said. "Attila the Great. It sounds like a magic act."

"I am Attila the Great, Shaman, Seer, Poet, Scourge of God," I said in my best epic voice. "You wanna see my magic horn?"

"You!!" she bleated, pummeling my chest playfully.

I pulled her to me and held her close.

She looked suddenly serious. "Promise me one thing," she said. "Promise you won't ever lie to me. I don't like to play games. I mean with stuff that really counts. Like us. I hate it when people say I love you and don't mean a word of it."

I nodded slowly but said nothing. "It's getting late," I said.

Long silence.

I caught her staring over my shoulder toward the top of the hill for signs of my brother. After a while, we both did. Nothing. All we saw was the black outline of pines spearing through a patch of sky.

I kissed her again. Millie said no one ever kissed her like that before. Her eyes were shiny.

"Hey!" came János's booming voice.

We looked up. Far up, my brother was waiting in a long winter coat and a Tyrolean hat.

As we got closer, Millie whispered that my brother looked like he was at least 30. She said she thought he was supposed to be only a couple of years older.

"Two and a half. Don't get into it with him."

János appeared polite, but a little grim and distant as we climbed into the family Chrysler. János said little and when he did it was in a heavy Hungarian accent. When we passed a brick church on Lorain Avenue, Millie said that was St. Angela Merici, where she went to grade school.

"You are Catholic?" János asked.

"Uhum," Millie said.

"We are Lutherans."

Millie said she was confused. She thought I was Catholic.

János glanced into the rearview suspiciously. Millie and me were huddled in a corner of the back seat. Nothing else was said. Millie must've sensed she said something wrong, because for the rest of the ride it was eerily quiet.

The next date was back to being unofficial. Another driving lesson. I hated having to depend on my brother or Gypsy. Millie got to borrow her mom's convertible, although this time the top would stay up. It was dipping into the teens and going down.

We were turning into a pretty steep curve on our way down the Valley. I took the corner nicely. "Nice," Millie said.

We were the only ones on the dark road. I remembered how to click on the brights. It took no time at all for me to find our spot and to kill the lights. We climbed into the back seat.

Millie was hardly settled when I kissed her with my tongue in that hungry way of mine, like I was about to eat right through her cheeks. My whole body heated up, not only my mouth. She let me unbutton her sweater and loosen her bra.

She was so, so...*white.*

I kissed her breasts. I kissed her stomach. Her girdle. I sighed. It was a hot sigh.

I was kneading the nylon of her girdle. I kissed her girdle, the girdle I hated. One kiss after another on the diamond reinforcement. But then I suddenly slowed down. I stopped.

I sat up, leaned my head against the back seat and stared ahead. The windows were fogging up. "Jesus, Millie. It's like kissing a glove."

Millie said she was sorry and put her head on my chest. My heart was going a mile a minute.

It took both of us to work the girdle off.

The panties stayed on.

She'd let me touch her, fondle her, kiss her wherever I wanted, but she wouldn't go all the way.

My hand wormed its way into her silk underpants. There was that fresh Christmas spice smell again. I said I wanted to see her. To feel her. I wanted them off. I wanted her.

"No," she said.

It was not a strong no. Not a definite no.

I caressed her soft white belly. My fingers were creeping down under the silk panties.

Millie moaned.

I felt the little hairs between her legs moisten.

She was touching me, too. Feeling how incredibly hard I was.

We shifted positions so I could lie on top of her. I was kissing her deeply when these headlights came on. Behind us.

The steamed-up glass made the lights swell to huge circles. I froze. I didn't just stop. I froze. Something came over me. Something physical. The muscles tensed. A current ran up my spine. My heart pounded. I was breathing hard like I was running a race. The headlights went off.

"Just another couple," Millie said, sitting up.

I couldn't take my eyes off the rearview. Millie said my eyes looked glassy. She could tell I was having trouble breathing.

I could barely get the words out: "Were we…followed?!"

Millie touched my arm. "What's wrong?" she asked.

"I don't know." And the crazy thing was I didn't.

"Are you afraid?"

"That's crazy," I said. There was an edge to my voice. "Why would I be afraid? You're the one who's afraid. Afraid to…do it."

Millie gathered her clothes.

"You're a prick teaser, you know that!"

"You can drive me home now," she said. Then she changed her mind. "No. I'll drive."

After my last driving lesson, I called Millie. I was sopping wet when I closed the door to the phone booth. "Hey, it's me," was all I said.

"I know it's you."

I stumbled over my words, but what came out was, "You're too easy." There was a little snake in the words.

For a long time, we said nothing. I heard the rain. Passing headlights swelled to huge circles. What was it with me? What was I afraid of? I was sure of only one thing, that it was easier to be angry than to be afraid.

"Is that what you think of what we did?" Millie asked. "You keep pushing me and pushing me to do it. And you think I'm easy?"

I let out a measured sigh and drew a line on the frosted glass. She hung up. I had to dig into my jeans' pocket for the roll of quarters. I was soaked. The paper roll had turned into mush. A few quarters slipped from my fingers. After a dial tone, I tried again, but there was no freaking answer.

So, this was it.

I didn't feel like going to my morning class and forged a note from my parents. (I wrote all my notes from home.) I didn't feel like school. The note said I had to go downtown to take my citizenship test which was bullshit. I was already a citizen, but I kept milking the excuse for as long as I could.

In exchange for Millie's wallet-size picture, I had given her one of my naturalization photos. That was before we broke up. I had inscribed the back with a one liner: "I ain't nothin' but a hound dog." Stupid as shit. She had encouraged me to write my own stuff. Mine. After a while, I did. The crazy girl had been my muse. As a poet, I'd come a long way from being nothing but a hound dog. At least I was writing my own shit now, not because I wanted to, but because I had to.

Instead of going to the high school, I took the Butternut Ridge bus to Westpark Rapid Station where I got on a train and rode the thirty-mile line from one terminal to the other, back and forth till it took up the school day. The trains were heated and I could be alone without anyone bugging me. It was a good way to avoid the girl who was breaking my heart, a good place to write my heart out. The poems were becoming darker and darker. Some were downright morbid. I thought the lines, "Love never stays/Love never lasts/So ring for me bells of the black mass," especially good, and was hurt much later when a teacher said they were terrible. Sentimental. I think *schmaltz* was the word he used. It meant dog shit.

For a whole week, I'd invent excuse after excuse to continue my marathon train rides to nowhere. Maybe my parents were right. Getting involved at my age was not the smartest thing in the world. It was my fault. Maybe I needed to change, get serious about school work, shower twice a day, quit smoking, change my religion, launch myself into space. What else? I wondered if she would ever take me back. I rushed to the phone, dialed and got the same answer. Not at home.

"Will she ever be home, Mr. Weiler?"

"For you? No," Mr. Weiler said.

Now I wished I never called. I wished I had never left Cathedral Latin and come to this frigging school just so Millie Weiler could break my heart. It ached alright, like a band around my chest. I couldn't sleep or eat right. All I did was smoke, and I did that non-stop. So much for quitting. When I went back to school the week after, I found out Millie's parents were trying to have her transfer out of government to a class offering conversational French. A friend told me that after graduation Millie was going to Paris to study art.

I caught up with her outside of school in the rain. Her hair was dripping wet. I told her I needed someone to stand up for me. I was going to be baptized a Catholic and I needed a godmother. "My original godmother had passed on," I said. "She was found frozen to death in her apartment in Budapest. But I don't want you to do it because you feel sorry for me."

She said she didn't feel sorry for me. She didn't feel anything for me.

"But all the time we spent together...?" I said.

She said a romance was supposed to be a happy time and she had been miserable.

"Miserable?"

"Yes. You kept pushing me to go all the way. And you called me a whore." She was crying.

We were both getting sopping wet now, but we didn't make any attempt to get out of the rain.

"I'm really sorry, Millie. I shouldn't've said those things. I don't know why I talked like that. Did I do it often?"

"Yes, you did. You made me feel cheap."

When I said I didn't remember, she reminded me about the time in the Valley. I was talking about diamond stars one minute, and tugging at the diamond reinforcement of her girdle the next. She didn't say it like that, but that's what she meant. What was that? And then I had the nerve to say she was easy.

I asked her if she was going to school in Paris. She said that was just her parents trying to impress the relatives. She was pretty sure she'd be staying put in Cleveland and end up going to the Art Institute on the East Side.

CHAPTER 4

"You know I can't do it unless we're married," Millie said over the telephone. We were back to talking on the phone but that was it. She would take me back but there would be conditions.

I brooded: "Conditions?"

"Yes. You've got to quit pestering me about doing it."

"Alright," I said in the tremulous voice I hated. "What else?"

"You'll have to come over my house and apologize to my Dad and tell him you've changed."

"Anything else?"

"Yeah. You wanna come over for some pizza tonight? It's not everyday I'm asked to be a godmother. Why do you want to become a Catholic anyhow? Why now? You never told me."

"All that Catholic schooling," I told Millie. "Guess they brain-washed me." I was glad I got to talk about this over the phone. I figured Millie's folks would make fun of me, which was still better than discussing it with my parents. My old man would throw me right out of the house for betraying the religion of our fathers. My father would say something like I was way too impressionable which translated to 'I was a quick sell-out.' He'd remind me that in Hungary I was an eager little Communist, saluting larger than life pictures of Marx, Lenin and Stalin, and now, I was falling on my knees before the Catholic Trinity—with the cult of Mary thrown in as a bonus.

No one would believe that ever since I was 12 I wanted to become a Catholic. I was even afraid to bring it up with Millie. She'd think I was some kind of fanatic. Converts usually were.

The thing was, the sisters at St. Emerich's told me I was missing many of God's graces and needed to devote myself heart and soul to God, especially since a 12-year-old was so vulnerable to temptation. I think that's the language they used. It was the flesh and the spirit dueling it to the death. That was about the time I began my spiritual exercises. Since cleanliness was next to godliness, I took daily baths. I kept my fingernails clean, made my bed, and placed my little black prayer book and my rosary on the night table, with a holy card as a page marker. Now and then, I'd get a holy card at school, beautiful cards with gilded edges, soft violet colors showing a sorrowful Holy Mother, her eyes looking up woefully. I thought then that there was more beauty in great sadness than in anything else, and a woman like Jesus' mother was the most tragic and most beautiful of God's creatures.

One day I brought Jesus home. I was almost 13. I remember winning the two-foot statue in the seventh grade by knocking down lead milk bottles with a softball at the school bazaar. It was going to be a gift for my mother. I was impressed by the statue's size. It was made of plaster and sprayed so that Jesus' eyebrows, eyelids and eyeballs were the same metallic gray. My mother was not touched by my gift. Maybe she had a bad day. My mother said Jesus had raccoon eyes and that the statue was cheap and vulgar. It was an American Christ that I brought home, she said. I was crushed and allowed myself to suffer. I seemed to welcome the pain, to savor it, to hoard it, to suffer like I imagined Jesus suffered. Although, come to think of it, it was not an American Jesus but a Japanese Jesus that I brought home. If my mother would've just looked at the bottom of the statue, it was there in plain English: *Made in Japan.*

I intensified my spiritual exercises. After my evening bath, I would put on my robe, go into the kitchen where I would prepare my chalice of grapes. I washed the grapes individually and with great ritual before putting them into a cup. While watching TV, I consumed them slowly, one by one, noting the cleanliness of my hands and body, my immaculate nails. I took communion every evening in my own special way, grapes instead of wine since I was a minor. The act made me feel serene in a way I couldn't explain. My hair was wet and combed. My family thought I was going through a phase. What they didn't know was that I was secretly training myself to be a holy man, a priest. Of course, the problem with becoming a priest was that I was the wrong religion, but that didn't stop me. I told Millie about this and it cracked her up.

Now I was 18. But I no longer wanted to become a priest. Millie said she was glad about that.

I went over to the Weilers with my hat in hand and my tail between my legs. When I told Mr. Weiler that I was going to be on my best behavior from now on, he barely looked up from his paper. "I should hope so," he said with a grunt. "Millie says you're getting baptized, is that right? What on earth for?"

"Dad!" Millie cut in.

"Protestant. Catholic," Mr. Weiler said. "It's all the same nonsense, if you ask me."

"The thing is I'm 18 now and I can choose for myself."

Mr. Weiler put down the paper and took his glasses off. "And it just so happens," he said, "that you're choosing the same religion as my daughter. Now that's a coincidence, if I ever saw one."

Mrs. Weiler came out with the pizza. "Come on, Rhett. He wanted to be a Catholic since he was a kid. He was an altar boy for crying out loud. Say something in Latin, Art."

"*Dominus vobiscum*," I said.

"There," said Mrs. Weiler.

"Oh, brother," Mr. Weiler said.

I was baptized Easter Sunday, two months to the day after I turned 18. In the presence of my godparents, I vowed to renounce Satan and all his works and all his display. My godparents were Gypsy, age 18, and Millie, age 17. I professed that I believed in Jesus Christ, God's only Son, Who was born into the world and suffered for us. I said I believed in the Holy Spirit, the Holy Catholic Church, the communion of saints, the forgiveness of sins, the resurrection of the body, and life everlasting. In short, I, Attila the Barbarian, the Scourge of God, renounced my pagan ways.

After my baptismal vows the priest sprinkled me with holy water. Following the ceremony, the three of us celebrated with a meal at Kentucky Fried Chicken, where we feasted on the Colonel's original recipe, coleslaw, corn on the cob, and mashed potatoes with gravy. Then we went for a ride. Millie and me that is. Gypsy begged off.

Millie was doing the driving this time. We decided to extend the ride by going down the Valley. It was such a fine spring day, the first sunny day in weeks. It was like a good omen. The leaves on the trees were a light green.

We didn't plan on stopping, but we did.

In my first confession only minutes before my baptismal vows, I confessed going down the Valley to engage in heavy petting. My confessor's response was a little heavy-handed. He forbade me to go down the Valley. Under the pain of sin. It didn't matter with whom. That sort of thing was reserved for the married state, the good priest said. Otherwise, I was committing the sin of human respect. That was a new one on me so I asked the priest about it. The priest said that was when you had greater love for man (in this case woman) than you had for God. It was a mortal sin, which meant I was risking my immortal soul by engaging in heavy petting with Millie.

If only she knew what I was putting on the line for her. I kissed her mouth, her hair, the tiny hairs on her neck, her shoulders, her breasts, with animal abandon. And I had these plans to take her on her first hayride the day after. It would be the Day of the Sprinkling, a great Hungarian holiday, and I would sprinkle her by pouring fragrant water on her hair. Who knew what would happen next? We held each other tight.

The priest had taught me to choose what was right, not what I felt was right. I had to act with what was between my ears, not what was between my legs. There was a huge difference. The problem was that Millie was just now touching what was between my legs and what was between my legs was growing to be a huge problem. And this huge problem was asserting itself only hours after I had renounced Satan and all his display.

I kissed Millie deeply. She kissed me back. I kissed her neck again and again, sucking on her skin, leaving a red hickey.

She pushed me away and checked herself out in the rearview. "Look what you did! You want me to meet your parents like this? Look at it. Why did you do that?"

The grand familia usually celebrated the traditional Day of the Sprinkling at Uncle Arthúr's bar and grill, but this year it was going to be special. My uncle bought a twenty acre farm twenty miles away in North Ridgeville, and he wanted everyone over, especially his favorite nephew who was almost a son to him. Let bygones be bygones.

I tried to bail out but it was to no avail once my family extended an invitation to Millie. "That American girl you've been hiding from us," was the way my father put it. The family was going to butcher a pig in her honor.

Dear God, I thought. Please don't. János and his big mouth. On the other hand, maybe it was time. Time Millie met the grand familia. Time my grand familia realized that the youngest man in the family was a man of taste. Maybe it wouldn't be so bad to show her off. Millie was a knockout, sure to knock their socks off.

"I'll think about it," I may have said.

"You're not ashamed of us, are you?" my mother said. "From what I hear, your uncle has horses on his farm. Does your American friend like to ride?" My mother was careful to say "friend" and not "girl-friend." There was a difference.

János put in his two cents. "Yeah," he said. "Uncle Arthúr even gives hayrides. Well, not him, personally, but his staff."

"Staff?"

My brother hedged. "The grooms. The horse people. You know."

"You mean the underpaid illegal aliens he's grooming to be the future Undertakers of America?"

"You got it."

"Who else is going to be there?"

"You. You're going to help us butcher the hog. Like back home. Was that fun or what? Then you can bring your girlfriend over for our traditional pig roast and go off on a moonlight hayride. I'll take care of the details myself."

My brother's rabidity caught me off guard. I was hoping against hope I wasn't smelling a disaster in the making. "Okay," I said, "let's do it. I'm ready. Let Millie see how we survived the last two thousand years on the steppes of Europe. I'm in the mood. We just finished *The Lord of the Flies* in school. Who else is going to be there?"

"Everybody."

By "everybody," my brother meant all the people that escaped with us from Hungary, plus a few add ons like Endre Szabó. It was time for East to meet West, I thought. Why not? Hey, with a hayride thrown in, it could even be groovy. I lit up a Camel offering one to János, who didn't smoke.

When I brought up the invitation to Millie, she said it was about time.

"I hope you like ham," I said.

I composed another note excusing myself from school, and gave it to Millie to hand to my homeroom teacher.

At the crack of dawn the next morning, me and my brother showed up at our uncle's farm. For most people, including my father, Monday was still a workday. My father didn't particularly care for butchering hogs, not because he was against cruelty to animals or anything, but because his arch-rival was so goddamm good at it. Besides he was raising his sons to be doctors, not butchers.

Uncle Arthúr's ranch was a brick affair off Sprague Road in the middle of Ohio farm country with its silos and ramshackle barns, endless fields of corn and soybean and shit. His nearest neighbor was a mile away. Since my uncle didn't have his name on the aluminum mailbox, my brother checked the numbers on our way in, just to make sure. A gravel path took us past a stretch of freshly plowed soil. It wasn't until we got closer that we realized the house was only partly finished.

We parked in the back by a field of new corn. A swaybacked brown horse was grazing a few feet away. Not exactly an Arabian stallion.

Uncle Arthúr came out in overalls and thermal undershirt with sleeves rolled up to the elbows. He gave me an unexpected bearhug as if he was greeting his long lost prodigal son. He said he was counting on me to be the star forward for the Hungarian Hunters. I told him I probably couldn't if I played in college next year. Playing for another team would violate NCAA rules.

"We wouldn't have to tell them, now, would we? I don't mean to be pigheaded, but I could use a good striker like you. Now, let's go and see the real pig."

We went directly to the pig pen to check out Golda. That was the name my uncle had given the blond, curly-haired sow. Her full name was Golda Mary, which was my uncle's perverted version of the Israeli foreign minister's name. Golda looked like she weighed a ton. My uncle said she should've been slaughtered earlier, but the dim-witted helpers couldn't get their act together. Stupid soccer players without green cards. Tradition like this was meant for family. Family only.

"Rain may be a problem," my uncle was saying. It was going to be slippery business.

We headed back to the house where the kitchen lights were on. My mother stayed over the night before to help with the preparations. She had made a pot of tea and strengthened it with good old *pálinka*. After the first sip, I let out a sigh, like all Hungarians worth their salt. It was good and strong. Rain or shine, I might get through this pig killing, after all.

The rain never got past the drizzle stage. We cleared a patch of ground between the pen and the silo.

Uncle Arthúr released the latch. The pig lurched out, sniffing along the fence. We rushed her, Golda squealed, knocked her bulk against the fence, leaving tufts of hair in the wire mesh. As it flew by, János gave it a swift kick on the flank.

"That's the way," my uncle coached. "Gotta break her stride."

The pig slipped in the mud. János clasped the butcher knife. He volunteered to be the one who had the honors. His first kill. János pounced on her, stabbing away blindly at the bristling fat neck. There was a blood-curling yowl. János was sprawling in the mud, clutching at his bloody hand. The poor sucker stabbed himself in the hand. Goddammit, János swore, then said it was nothing.

"My ass," Uncle Arthúr said. He took out a handkerchief from his overalls and gave János's hand a quick wrap. "Baptism by blood," he said. "Good as new. Now go and finish the job."

The three of us fell on the dazed and bleeding hog like savages. I held her by the hind legs, which were jerking, but I held them fast.

János was there with the pan to catch the blood gushing from the hog's neck.

Once we drained the blood, we heaved Golda squarely on her back onto where my uncle had spread hay. We rolled the hog on her side, tossed a match into the hay and watched the wind fan the flames into a bonfire.

I lit one of my Camels by sticking my chin close to the flames. I stood up and took a deep, satisfying drag. My mother came out to inspect our work. She brought a pot of scalding water to clean the pig once all the hair was singed off. She had the jug of *pálinka* with her. We each took a swig and let out a sigh.

Uncle Arthúr said the smell of burning pork was making him hungry and he hoped breakfast was on the table.

"What do you think?" my mother said.

It wasn't long before we planted ourselves in the steamy kitchen to have some boiled blood and onions. I couldn't help but wonder what my American girlfriend would think of these rations. Not exactly oatmeal, but it did stick to your ribs in its own way.

It took several pots of scalding water to clean Golda. Uncle Arthúr knelt as he scrubbed between the swollen knuckles with a laundry brush. We turned the animal belly up. Where she was singed to a pink brown my uncle made an incision. The blood underneath the skin was black. The intestines were the first to be taken out. They were to be washed for sausage casings.

My uncle was working deep inside Golda when he said all "isms" were full of shit. He had a habit of talking while he worked. More like lecturing. And his nephews were a captive audience. "Isms" he said, "breed each other, then screw each other." It was no secret that Communism was the handiwork of capitalist pigs. Everything was a question of economics. And Jews. What followed was my uncle's familiar conspiracy theory about Jews. It all started with the Old Testament. The Jews were the real racists. Didn't they kill all the people in the countries they invaded? And burn their livestock. Their crops? Did they teach us that in the fancy schools we went to? He didn't think so. "What about the Rosenbergs?"

"My girlfriend knows about them," I said. "We studied about them in government class. She knows about Julius and Ethel Rosenberg pissing away the atomic bomb to the Russians."

My uncle was impressed. "Oh yeah? What about that other Rosenberg? Dr. Jakab Rosenberg. Your father's nemesis."

Me and my brother exchanged glances. We knew all about our father and Dr. Jakab Rosenberg, but we never brought it up. János tried changing the subject. Fat chance. Not only would Uncle Arthúr not let it go, he worked himself into a rage: "As far as I'm concerned your father did the right thing. Those sons of bitch Jews had it coming."

My mother overheard. She said, "More work and less talking." She had to boil the intestines, she didn't want to be late with dinner for their American guest. The sausage was going to be on the table on time, for a change.

Uncle Arthúr let out a mocking laugh. "Don't you worry about that. She's more interested in your son's sausage than this old pig's."

János snickered. My mother smiled and said, "You're just going to have to watch your mouth."

The rain had stopped and the sun was setting, leaving blotches of red and purple on the horizon when Millie pulled up the gravel driveway. I went out to her car as she parked. She smiled. I didn't. I thought Millie was overdressed in her canary yellow mohair suit. She had her hair poofed professionally, and she looked more like a country western singer than a serious student. I didn't know what to make of the look. I knew it would grate on my old-fashioned parents, who didn't think girls should wear lipstick. Millie's lips were a lovely metallic red, as usual. And her large blue eyes stood out more than ever with their Cleopatra outlines. But today they started to bug me just a little. I was seeing her through my mother's eyes, and whatever attracted me to my American girl was turning into something not so very nice. If only she didn't wear those stockings with the seams down the back. They usually drove me crazy. But what would my mother and father think? God!

I did my best, but I couldn't hide the fact that I was freaked by her getup.

"Don't you like the way I look?" Millie asked. She looked hurt. "I wore this for Easter."

"It's a hayride."

"I'm meeting your parents. I want to make a good impression."

My answer was a willful sigh.

"Well, what is it?"

"It's the yellow," I said, referring to the color of her suit. "To Hungarians, yellow is a color of illness. It's a bad omen, that's all."

"You know what? You're a bad omen. If your family's like that, I don't think I want to meet them. You think you look so great with that stupid tie? Look, if you don't think I'm good enough to meet your family, I can go home now."

"I didn't mean that."

"What did you mean?"

"I don't know."

Millie said I'd better have a cigarette. My eyes were turning black. What was the big deal, anyhow?

I couldn't have been more off. The family loved her. They ooh'd and ah'd over how great she looked.

"Oh, she's a looker," my mother said in Hungarian. "Look at those blue eyes. "Tell her she's pretty, son."

"You know that much English."

"You are a pretty girl, yes?" said my mother to Millie.

I was amazed my mother's hair was poofed up like Millie's.

My father bowed and kissed Millie's hand. He wore a starched white collar, tie and suit—and a gold-plated wrist watch under his sleeve which he flashed. "*Wilkommen*," he said, beaming at Millie.

Millie was all smiles. She whispered that my family was perfectly nice. What was all the fuss about?

My brother came up with his hand wrapped in gauze. After a nervous hello, he retreated. He was the only one who knew about my recent betrayal of the faith of our father(s).

Uncle Arthúr was impressed. When he shook Millie's hand, he said she had delicate hands. Too delicate for work. "I'm serious," he said. "She must be an artist. Do me a favor," he said to me in Hungarian, "Tell her never ever to wash dishes. She must keep hands like this out of dishwater. Leave that kind of work to foreigners. Like us."

Endre Szabó was there as well, with his new wife, an import straight from a village in Hungary. It looked like Endre was dying to cut in. "What do you know about art?" he said to my uncle in a voice that was already well-oiled by good old Hungarian *pálinka*. "What do any of you know about artists' hands?"

Since his recent wedding, Endre had cut back on the booze, but today it looked like he was making an exception. His slicked-back hair curled up by his nape. He made a desperate attempt to look dashing, and he almost pulled it off. The trouble was with his dentures. They wobbled when he spoke. The man seemed to have taken a perverse interest in my date, and made no bones about it. And in his new wife's presence. I quickly ushered Millie out of the room, but not far enough. We were still within earshot. Endre was telling his wife in Hungarian that the girl was wasting her time with me. I was too young to know what to do with lips like that. "Shhh," his wife tried to muzzle him, "you're drunk," to which Endre replied, "You're just jealous, you old goat."

Man, this Szabó guy was persistent. He was stalking us with a drink, spilling most of it as his wife tugged at his sleeve. Endre wanted to know if I had sprinkled her yet.

"Don't listen to him," his wife said apologetically.

Me and Millie continued our retreat to what looked like the dining room.

An old ping-pong table was covered nicely with a white tablecloth. My mother was placing a porcelain soup tureen in the center. "Everybody sit now," she said. She pointed to a fold-up chair for Millie. "You sit here, honey. Your hair looks so nice and full. Is it professional? I am sorry, my English."

"Tell your mother her English is fine."

"Why don't you?" I said.

"Your English is fine."

Everybody sat around the table now. My father was pouring wine. "What would your lady friend like to drink?"

Millie said, "Coke? With a little ice?"

"They don't drink Coke around here," I said to Millie.

My uncle was quick to follow up. He had a regular theory about Coca-Cola. And ice. He said, in Hungarian of course, that you really had to be dumb to pay money for a mixture of tar, rain-water, and soda. As for the ice, it usually took up three quarters of your glass, and you were paying for ice instead of soda. My uncle wanted me to translate what he said to Millie.

I didn't. Instead, I said it made sense to forget the ice. With all the cavities and metal fillings in our family.

"I see your son hasn't lost his touch," my uncle said to my mother.

"A little Hungarian wine, then?" my father asked. "Tell her it's called the Blood of the Bull. Translate! Tell her it's called that because the Turks who occupied Hungary for 150 years beginning with the 15th century—"

"Get on with it, man," Endre Szabó interrupted rudely. Alcohol was making him reckless.

My father ignored him. "Being Moslems, the Turks could not drink alcohol. It was against their religion. So, the Hungarians tricked them by telling them it was not alcohol but the blood of the bull. Well, to make a long story short, the Turks were a lot easier to deal with after a little alcohol. Unlike some in the present company."

Loud guffaws. Laughter.

"Hear! Hear!" Endre said.

I told Millie the man was an idiot. "Oh yeah," she whispered. "He's something else."

Suddenly Millie looked horrified. She pointed to her soup. There was something in her soup.

Part of the pig's jaw. Teeth and all.

"What's that?" she said, her face frozen in horror.

Everybody laughed.

My father was clinking his spoon against his glass to reclaim order.

"János's idea of a joke," I said as I removed the teeth from Millie's soup. I looked around. Where was that crazy brother of mine?

"Tell her she's lucky she didn't get the pig's—" Uncle Arthúr said without finishing his sentence. My mother cut him off with a look. "The poor girl is from the city," she said. "Leave her alone. Not nice to tease."

My father was still standing with a glass of red wine in his hand. Finally, he made a toast. "The Day of the Sprinkling," he said, "has been our national custom even before St. Stephen converted all the Hungarian tribes to Christianity in the year 1000. Some in the civilized world still regard us as barbarians. Barbarians! Who's the barbarian now, bloody Christ?" He didn't expect an answer. With the exception of Millie, we all knew that by "barbarians" he meant the Russians. "The real barbarians are the Red Army who swept across Hungary to kill innocent men, desecrate women and to defile the graves of our fathers."

"And to take away your job," Uncle Arthúr said.

My father reached for a cigarette with trembling fingers. He was beet red. "I had a royal seat on the royal bench," he hissed at my uncle. "When you didn't even have a toilet seat in your outhouse."

"That's right. That's how I like it. Out in nature, with the flies. I don't take royal shits like you do, I just want to know—and those present may want to know—why we Hungarians are so obsessed with sprinkling. Why? It's a pagan rite, isn't it? To say it's about fertility is a bit too sanitized for my taste. Think about what it really is. Why don't we just call it what it is and be done with it? To do otherwise is downright barbarian, if you ask me."

"I'm not asking you," my father said.

My mother said, "Quit arguing. It's not polite."

Uncle Arthúr pounded on the table. "It's symbolic intercourse!" he said.

My mother rolled her eyes and thanked my uncle for taking her appetite away.

"What's going on?" Millie wanted to know.

Endre opened his mouth again. This time he was slurring his words. His new wife's jaw dropped. Endre was saying that it was all a lot of bullshit. Hungarians *were* barbarians. St. Stephen screwed up. He sold out his pagan brothers to the fucking Pope. "All our beautiful pagan artifacts fucking destroyed! All we got left is this fucking sprinkling shit."

"He is so drunk," I was telling Millie.

She whispered that she could see that. "Is it okay to ask them about the horses. How many horses does your uncle have on his farm? I didn't see any when I came in."

"What?"

"Horses. Horses."

My uncle wanted me to tell the girl that Hungarians were the greatest horse riders in the world. With their bows and arrows they were the scourge of Europe.

"Horseshit," Endre Szabó said. "That's why we lost every war."

"I don't believe this," my father said. He was on his third glass of wine. He lifted his glass and asked Millie in eloquent broken English whether she was familiar with Franz Liszt's *Hungarian Rhapsody*.

I answered for her by saying that Liszt didn't make the Top Ten this week.

"What about Bach? Ask her if she speaks German?"

"Father, please," I said. "She speaks English. American English."

"Alright. Alright," my father said. "Is it permitted if I ask about her father? About what he does for a living?"

I translated.

"He's a salesman."

"Good for him," my uncle said with absurd enthusiasm. Then in Hungarian he said, "That's what this country's all about. Selling and peddling. Lying and cheating. Got to feed the evil empire."

By this time my father was furious. "Arthúr, do you mind? I haven't been able to say a word without some asinine interruption."

"That's right," my mother said. "Can't we act civilized, for a change? We're ruining a perfectly good dinner. Attila, I mean Art, I want you to apologize to this poor girl for me. Tell her we don't know how to behave."

"It's fine," I said.

János came in but only long enough to tell me the hay was ready, but he couldn't find the damned horse. But he was working on it.

"No, it's not fine," my father continued where he left off. "It's not fine. We are a civilized people. We are educated."

"I told her you were a royal judge," I said to placate him.

"Tell her," my father said, "that just because we don't speak the language we are not stupid people."

"She knows that."

"No, let me finish. Tell her the Communists took away everything we had. We had a beautiful life in our country before the dark forces of atheistic Communism—"

"Let the poor girl eat already. Everybody eat now," my mother ordered.

And eat we did. We literally pigged out on pork paprikash, stuffed cabbage, red sausage, rice sausage, black blood sausage. My uncle and Endre shoveled down their food. They had great fun gnawing, slurping, chomping, making noises like dogs under a table. When we ate, there was usually no talking. Hungarians didn't discuss things between sips of wine and polite bites. Eating was serious business and the pace furious. Millie was a sport and tried a little bit of everything. Now and then, my mother asked, "You like?" Millie usually had her mouth full and just nodded.

We were still eating when my mother brought out dessert. Ground chestnuts mixed with rum and topped with whipped cream.

My mother asked, "Your family, honey. Where do they come from?"

"From Fairview Park," Millie said.

"She's German," my father said. "Weiler is a German name."

"Are you German, honey?"

Millie dabbed her mouth with a paper napkin. "Actually, I'm American."

That's when János came to the rescue. He was signaling to us from across the room. I excused myself and Millie. My mother said she'd have something special for us when we got back. "Don't be too long."

Outside, it was already dark. János took us out back to a shed and turned on a flashlight. Eight sticks of red sausage, two slabs of salt pork, one curing in garlic, still pink. Dangling from the ceiling was the pig's bulbous stomach, stuffed with ears, cheeks, lips, tail, gum, and whatever else could be chopped into good old headcheese. Hanging on a hook next to it was the scrubbed and gutted carcass of the other half of the pig.

"This is it? You called us out for this?" I said to János.

He lit one of my Camels. "Mother said Millie should take some to her parents."

"Oh God no," Millie said.

János looked hurt. He told me he still needed a hand heaving that half a hog into the car.

Somehow, my injured brother and me hoisted the half carcass into the trunk of the Chrysler. János slammed the trunk and told us to follow him.

We went down a steep flight of stairs to the basement. János flicked on the light. The lone bulb was just enough to light up the enormous barrel.

From a hole on top coiled a rubber hose. János handed the hose to me. I took the hose into my mouth. Nothing. I sucked harder. Still nothing came. Then an unexpected surge filled my mouth and nose. I coughed. It was a mixture of wine and regurge.

"You alright?" Millie asked.

I nodded. "Wanna try it?"

"Not me."

"Chicken."

Wine trickled from the end of the hose. My brother stopped it with his thumb so we didn't waste any precious Blood of the Bull.

János and me took turns pulling on the hose until we were good and light-headed. And my brother felt no pain in his hand. Now, János decided, we were ready to check out that hayride.

We stumbled into a dark ramshackle building with part of the roof missing. You could see a patch of starry sky. There were no horses, no wagons. Just an old Ford pick-up loaded with hay.

"*Voila!*" János said. He told us he gave up looking for the horse and fixed up the pick-up instead. The only problem was the pick-up had a flat and there was no spare.

Millie was stunned. Disappointed. She expected a real hayride. She asked János where his date was. "Art told me you were bringing a date. Where are the others?"

They were on their way, János said. As for his date, he had to call her and tell her he was out of commission because of his hand. He held up his wrapped hand. But now, he said, he was sorry he called it off. It was pretty nice out here.

"You must be kidding," Millie said.

János shrugged. "Oh well," he said. "I'd make the best of it. Make hay while the moon shines and all that." With that he sauntered off.

"He had a little too much wine," I said.

"Yeah? What's your excuse? No one else is coming, are they?"

"They got lost."

"I'm sure."

I climbed into the bed of the pick-up and fell in. I rolled around in the hay to show Millie how much fun it was. Fresh, sweet, hay. No manure.

I was so desperate it made Millie laugh. "Alright," she said. She could pretend to be having fun, too. As she climbed up, I offered her a hand. She took it. I yanked her in and she fell on me. We rolled around in the hay. I was on top of her kissing her neck. I pressed myself into her and she responded. I ran my hand up the seams of her nylon stockings.

There was that girdle again. The girdle I hated. It was like a chastity belt. Unnatural. Unnatural to cut off the circulation like that. I massaged the band of bare thigh between hose and girdle.

I unzipped my trousers and rubbed myself against the girdle.

Our kisses deepened. Her back arched to meet my body. We were rolling and rocking, and it wasn't long before I ejaculated into the prickly straw.

Millie did not look entirely happy.

There was straw in her hair, on her canary-yellow suit, under the skirt, between her legs. Her stockings were shredded. She would have to take them off and said she hoped no one would notice.

I uttered a sheepish sorry and helped pick off the straw.

"God, Art," she said. "You got stuff on my new suit." She was on the verge of tears. "Damn it all anyhow. What's your family going to think of me now?"

I didn't say anything, but my body did. A cold nausea rumbled through my chest.

We headed back to the house in cold silence. She wouldn't let me put my arm around her. She wanted to go home. Now.

My mother was busy doing the dishes when we squeezed through the door. She smiled at us. "The *palachinta* is still hot. Come, come. Before they are all gone."

Palachinta was another family favorite. Thin pancakes rolled like crepes and stuffed with hot cottage cheese, and sprinkled with powdered sugar.

I begged Millie to stay for another round of dessert. Everyone was seated exactly as we had left them, except for Endre Szabó, whose head was face down on the table.

My mother piled our plates high with *palachinta*, poured brandy on top and lit it. The blue flame lasted a few seconds, the crepes were piping hot.

"Tell your friend it gives it a special taste."

"Oh, I'm pretty full. Can you tell her I'm stuffed?" Millie said.

"Just try one," I said. I felt full myself and had to force it. My stomach was a seething mass wedged between my diaphragm and my lungs. I could barely breathe.

My mother said she didn't have to. She was probably tired. Then my mother changed the subject by asking Millie if her mother was born in America.

Millie said her mom was born in Cleveland, but she's of Irish, French, and Russian descent.

"That's nice," my mother said.

"What about your father? Your papa?"

"Oh, my Dad. He's American, too. His family originally came from Germany. His grandfather was a rabbi."

Endre Szabó burst out in a loud guffaw.

"It's true!" Millie said. "My great grandfather's name was Schlomo. Rabbi Schlomo Weiler."

Suddenly it was quiet. The kind of quiet where you could hear a bowstring tighten.

"*Zsidó*." Uncle Arthúr said. It was the Hungarian word for "Jew."

"What's wrong?" Millie said.

"They think you're a Jew."

"Well, tell them I'm not. I was baptized a Catholic, like you. And what if I was?"

It was like a bomb had gone off and we were both at ground zero, our ears still ringing. My mother's voice sounded faint and distant. She was saying in Hungarian, "But the girl has such beautiful blue eyes."

Once Millie and me were on our way in her mom's car, top up because it looked like it was going to rain again, we didn't speak for the longest time. I was so freaking bloated I undid my belt. I must've swallowed a lot of air on top of everything else. All that sausage crap wasn't agreeing with me. Out of the blue, Millie said, "You know I won't do it unless I'm married."

"You could've said something about your father being Jewish and everything."

She looked straight ahead as she spoke. "For Pete's sake, what does that have to do with anything? My Dad's not religious. He eats pork. He eats ham and bacon all the time. Did your parents think I didn't take the sausage and all that because we're Orthodox Jews or something? For crying out loud."

"I just wished you could've told me, that's all."

"What difference does it make? Unless it makes a difference to you."

"You don't understand."

"No, I don't."

Silence, again.

"I want to know where you stand," Millie said. She took her eyes off the road and looked at me. "I'm serious. I want to know."

I told her I wasn't sure.

Wrong answer. The tires came to a screeching stop as she pulled off to the side. "You had better tell me what you think, Buster."

"God, Millie."

She turned off the ignition and blew some air out through pursed lips. I looked at Millie closely. I picked a piece of straw we missed from her hair. I told Millie she was right. I was old enough to think for myself now. Yeah, I thought to myself. I was old enough to drink beer. Old enough to choose my own religion. Old enough to renege on my old religion. Old enough to renege on my new religion. And on the same freaking day! Old enough to break my father's heart, old enough to break my uncle's heart. Old enough to serve Uncle Sam. Old enough to be wanted by Uncle Sam. Old enough to serve my new country. Old enough to wage war against my old country if need be. Old enough to fight in a hell-hole called Vietnam. Old enough to follow this Jewish girl to hell. Yeah, I was old enough to think for myself.

"Are you alright?" Millie said. "You're all flushed."

Cars swished past us in the rain, some blowing their horns, but I didn't care. "I think I love you, Lyudmilla Weiler," I said.

It was suddenly very quiet.

"I'm not anything like my family," I said. "Not like any one of them. I'm different. Since I was a kid, I fought them at every turn. I was a pain in the ass, defiant as shit. Sometimes I felt like a freaking little Judas. I guess it was my way of thinking for myself, without knowing it. It wasn't until now, until you brought it up, that I realized all this shit. That I could like what I like, not what they like. And, yeah, to hate what they like. It was always what they thought, never what I thought. What do *I* think? It makes no frigging difference to me what you are. Jew or Zulu. I love you. I want to be with you. Do you understand that? You don't have to understand me as long as you understand that. I choose you. You! You actually listen to me. You think they listen to me? I mean really listen? You make me feel good. They make me feel crappy about myself. I'm pissed all the time. They resent the fact that they can't control me like a robot. Man, do they hate that. And because I love you, they hate you. I can't accept that. Can't and won't. Sooner or later they'd want me to give you up. It's not going to happen. For all I care, they can bugger themselves in the ass with their bullshit racism. Jew, Jew, Jew. That's all they talk about. Wasting all their time obsessing about Jews. Their scapegoat for everything. From taking away my father's job to crucifying Christ. You were right about my old man being a Nazi. The man idolizes Hitler. He has books at home you wouldn't believe. And he thinks the Jews are out to get him. Because…because he had these three Jews executed."

"What??"

"My father sentenced three Jews to death by hanging."

"Oh my God!"

"Yeah. When he was a royal judge. They were Communist Jews who committed treason. One man's name was Dr. Jakab Rosenberg. Remember when you asked me who Dr. Rosenberg was? I couldn't tell you then. I just wasn't ready. I thought you'd hate me."

"For what? For being the son of a Nazi? You can't help what your father did. You didn't do it. What about your mother?"

"She's just as bad. They all think the same way, I swear. She's not going to like you either. She'll never see you as a person. As someone I love. She'll say terrible things like you're a whore and stuff like that. Hurtful stuff. When I, when I see you through her eyes, that's when I say lousy things I don't mean. Things like you're easy and stuff. I can just see her now. She's so happy your father's a Jew, because now she thinks it's over. Kaput. She wants to be the one to pick out a nice Hungarian girl for me from the village. Someone who can cook, bake, and play the piano. Someone she can manipulate. She hates people who have their own minds. She only knows how to manipulate. She doesn't know how to love."

My voice cracked. Millie touched my hand. "I love you," she said. We held each other for a long time. Until a police cruiser pulled up behind us, lights flashing. "It's the fuzz," I said, surprising myself. No heart pounding this time. It must've been letting all this heavy stuff out. I felt easy. Like I could breathe. That's when I realized my belt was undone and my fly open. As the cop asked for Millie's license he looked into the passenger side. Millie caught on, and we could barely keep a straight face as she handed over her license. So far, no problem. Then the officer spoke up: "You kids ever hear of the Valley? It's not as busy as Lorain Avenue. Now, scoot." He let us off. No ticket. Not even a warning.

We took this as a sign. Instead of going straight home we decided to drive down the Valley. We were laughing about my fly being open and all that, but after a while Millie got serious. She wanted to know if I noticed the policeman's nametag. I didn't. Well, it turned out she did. Gabriel. It was the angel Gabriel. I told her to give me a break. She was all business. "Come on," she said. "I believe in these things."

I said it was okay.

She parked by a little stone bridge in a secluded part of the Valley. We pushed our seats back. But we just talked. I told Millie how the priest "forbade" me to go down the Valley. "This whole Catholic thing is getting me down. I'm so frigging confused."

"Where's the sin in going down the Valley? We only kissed. We didn't do anything wrong. I can't stand the way the Church wants to control everything. I'll tell you something, Art, I'm not crazy about organized religion."

"I'm not, either." I put my hand on her thigh and kept it there.

Millie removed my hand gently. "It doesn't mean I don't believe in God," she said. "I do. I consider myself very spiritual. When I was a kid in grade school, I wanted to be a nun."

"And I wanted to be a priest. Did I tell you?"

"But you were the wrong religion."

"I know. How 'bout you?"

"I could've become a nun. My Dad tortured me about that for the longest time. He was such a jerk. But then I discovered I liked boys. Then the nuns told me my father was going to hell because he was a Jew. It didn't make any sense. God was supposed to love everybody. I mean, I'm not crazy about my father. But I wouldn't send him to hell. And I'm not better than God. The truth is, I don't like all the rules and regulations. But I love God. I don't need some priest or rabbi telling me I can't have God without them. I mean, do they own God? Sometimes I get so angry. And frustrated. You think I didn't want you as much as you wanted me in that stupid pick-up? I wasn't angry about the stupid straw. And I wasn't angry at you. I was just angry because I wanted you. I wanted you so bad but I couldn't have you."

She dropped her hands. Her eyes were filled with tears. "What are we going to do?"

I told her I loved her.

"I know you do. But we can't just run away somewhere. You have all that school ahead of you. God, how many years?"

"Eleven."

"We're so young. If only we weren't so young." Millie bit her lip.

I was 18 now, old enough to get drafted but not old enough to get married. Even if I wanted to. The laws of Ohio did not allow it without parental consent. It was now me comforting Millie, wiping her tears away. I took another piece of straw out her hair and kissed her on the cheek. Her skin was flaming hot.

Millie said, "You know I can't do it till we're married. What if, what if we married ourselves? Just you and me. And God. As long as God knows, it's alright. We'll keep it a secret. Until you become a doctor. We'll make it legal then."

Her eyes were shiny as she said these things. I looked into her eyes and got lost in them. I did not want to find my way back. I wanted her to hold me there, where her soul was, where I felt safe. I was really afraid. More afraid than on No-Man's Land when me and my father were in the cross-hairs of Russian guns. More afraid than when me and my godmother got caught in that freaking crossfire by the church. I was scared shitless of a love that would defy parents, priests, churches, afraid of a girl who insisted on loving me the way she did. And I was afraid of myself for having the balls to defy and to defile my family. Because I'd rather go to hell with this girl than to heaven with my so-called holy family. Because no one was going to wear down my spirit, my love for this American girl. It felt that good to be lost in her eyes. And I was lost, man, I was really lost.

I told her I wanted her, no matter what. We didn't need anyone's approval. Anyone's. "Shit, we'll marry ourselves!"

Millie let that sink in before she spoke up. "You're not just saying that, are you? Because if you are, I won't go through with it. I mean, this is forever. You can't get a divorce from God."

CHAPTER 5

We exchanged vows on May 26, 1965, on a little stone bridge deep in the Valley and in the sight of God. A brook ran under the bridge, surrounded by these huge trees. They were like tall arches reaching up to the sky. Columns of our cathedral. It was true. God was there with us, as certain as the yellow sunlight coming in through the leaves.

Millie wore a sleeveless blue dress. She said it was jersey. All I knew that it was soft to my touch. Her hair was swept up like a ballet dancer's. A necklace with an ivory heart hung from her neck. A gift from me. She knew it was special, carved from an ivory chip I'd been carrying around with me forever. It was all that was left of the horn that saved my life. She fished out a prayer book from her shoulder bag. Her childhood *Saint Joseph Daily Missal.* The pages were marked, the marriage vows highlighted.

"I will take you, Lyudmilla Weiler, for my wife, to have and to hold, from this day forward."

I groped in my pocket for the 18 dollar silver ring. When I finally got it out I had to shake it to get rid of the lint. I put it on her finger and gave it a squeeze. One size fits all, so I made it smaller to fit her tiny finger. The ring had black enameled Chinese symbols for joy and happiness, and was shaped like a coiled snake.

"And I will take you, Art Nagy, for my husband, to have and to hold, from this day forward." She put a silver wedding band on my finger.

With a trembling voice, I read from another part of the prayer book that my wife shall be like a fruitful vine in the recesses of my home.

Millie told me afterwards the marriage in the Valley was the first time she ever had what you'd call a mystical experience. She felt as if God had put His hand on her shoulder and said, "You did good." It confirmed she did the right thing, that I really was the one for her. God had blessed our union.

The only remaining problem was that the "recesses" of my home was not even under construction. We still lived under our parents' roof.

Our wedding night was spent at *Putt-A-Round* working at her father's miniature golf course, a little side-business he invested in three years ago. We had trouble keeping our hands off each other once Millie turned the key and we stepped over the threshold of the little red clubhouse. Only a few customers that night. So much the better. We spent our time kissing.

This would be the night.

By the time Millie closed up, we were both insanely hungry for each other. I helped her roll down the shutters and lock up. We placed mats on the floor and one of those Indian blankets. Millie slipped off her summer dress, no girdle this time, just her silk underpants. They came off easily. She was naked for me, except for the ivory heart necklace. We lay next to each other on the blanket. My trembling hand explored her body. Millie had sneaked one of her Dad's condoms into her purse. There was an awkward moment when we stopped our love play to fool with the condom. I seemed to have trouble getting it on. I made the mistake of unrolling it first.

"You can't put it on like a sock," she said.

I felt like an idiot. Millie seemed to know just how it was done. What did that mean? I was too excited to worry about it now. But later, and not much later, I'd be mulling it over in my head. Over and over.

I didn't like the feel of the rubber. This was the first time I ever used one. This was my first time, period. As for my new wife, I wasn't so sure. Where did she hear that sock business? What did she know about rolling or unrolling condoms? Oh, what did it matter? I was lost in her.

Inside of her. She loved me inside her. She was moaning sweetly in the little Hungarian I taught her. She was saying, "*Jó. Jó. Jó.*" It meant, "Good. Good. Good."

This beautiful girl was loving what I was doing to her. She wanted me to go deeper and deeper into her and to became a part of her. When my body shuddered, she held me. We released each very slowly.

"Was it as good for you as it was for me?" she asked.

"Better."

She smiled. Her eyes looked sleepy, content.

I noticed there wasn't much blood at all. But I was not going to ask about it. Not now. Maybe not ever. What did I know? I didn't even know how to roll on a condom. Suddenly, and just for a second, I was terrified. That I'd been tricked. That I'd lost my soul to a beautiful siren who was secretly laughing at me. Then I thought of God. His blessing. Then I thought of what she said about putting on a condom like a sock.

Once we were dressed, Millie sent me to the drugstore for some sodas while she finished the paperwork connected with closing.

In the drugstore, I noticed I felt different. The light seemed overly bright, the stuff on the shelves too vivid, as if they had too much color. It scared me that my eyes felt like they were too sensitive to the light. There was something vulnerable about me now and I didn't like it. The first thing I did outside the store was to fire up a cigarette. That seemed to help some.

Millie and me had a Coke with a little *pálinka* I smuggled from home. At one point, I was conscious of holding my drink and my cigarette in one hand, just like Mr. Weiler. I felt better already. It was better than feeling stupid and sensitive.

Late that night, Millie called to tell me her parents had driven by the golf course to check on us and caught us kissing. Her father was furious. He chewed her out and called her a whore. She said she was relieved that's all they saw. Anyway, she was fired and so was I.

We did it every chance we had, when and wherever we could. We sometimes did it in her mother's convertible under the stars, sometimes under our parents' roof, sometimes right under their noses. When there was no one at home at her house, she'd greet me at the door in a negligee, and we'd run upstairs and do it in her bed.

I got back at Millie's father for being mean by smoking his cigarettes and using up his condoms. Her Dad bought them both by the carton even though he was diabetic and impotent.

When Millie sent me an anniversary card to the house celebrating our first month as man and wife, I panicked. The card read, "To My Hubby." Just in case I forgot. I was a husband. Did I want to be a husband? The husbands I knew were all old and creepy like my father and like Millie's father, Rhett. Like my Uncle Arthúr. No, I didn't want to be like any of them. But I wanted to be inside Millie. In fact I was obsessive about it.

We kept on doing it in the bushes after a dance at Legion Hall and had a huge laugh trying to pull the burrs from Millie's fuzzy sweater. Graduation day, the last minute, at my house on the living room floor while my parents and brother were driving around, looking for a parking space. We almost missed our own graduation. Worries about Millie's dress and mussed-up hair.

We did it after the Senior Prom, on the kitchen floor, with her parents upstairs. After the Post Prom and after everything else.

Almost every single day of our summer vacation. The closer we got to the end of summer, the more we saw of each other, the more intense our lovemaking.

I'd been accepted to Cleveland State University right here in town. My parents said that was all they could afford. The real reason was they wanted to keep tabs on me, to make sure I didn't assimilate and do something stupid like dilute my blood.

Millie's parents were going to send her away to art school, where she was going to live in a girls' dorm.

We were both freaked about the separation. I wanted to do it all the time now but Millie was afraid of getting pregnant and getting caught by her parents. Bonnie, her dog, was our sentry on the back porch. Still Millie was nervous, and couldn't relax.

"Bonnie's out there," Millie kept telling me, but I knew it was more for her benefit than mine. Bonnie would bark at the slightest noise.

We sat around her dining room table, nibbling on Millie's left-over birthday cake. I whined that she was more interested in the cake than in me. Within days she'd be moving to the east side of Cleveland for art school, and I would be starting college at Cleveland State University downtown. We began fighting about not getting enough of each other. I said she didn't love me enough, and she was anxious to prove she did, in the usual way. No one was at home, and there wasn't much time before Millie's parents came back, but I insisted. We were doing it right on the dining room table when the door to the dining room flared open.

It was Millie's mom. She made a gagging sound and slammed the door shut.

Millie threw me off her, pulled down her skirt, then burst out crying. Through the door her mom, trying to control her voice, said we must've lost our heads. That I had better go home, and that Millie had better go upstairs. Her Dad was not going to be very happy when he finds out.

I zipped up my jeans and held Millie awkwardly. I swore I'd never leave her. Millie pushed me away. Her mom was right, she said. I'd better leave before her Dad got back. Millie didn't kiss me. She had to get me out of there. "Go! Now! You don't know my Dad. He's liable to kill you!!"

I left the house, but not the neighborhood. I lay low among some tall grass nearby and kept an eye on her house, in case Millie needed me. I watched as her father's car pulled in and he went into the house. After more than an hour of quiet, I walked home.

My brother János intercepted me in our driveway. He said we'd better walk around the block and talk. The Weiler house was *verboten*, he said. I could forget it. If I as much as go near the house, old man Weiler was going to bash my head in with a baseball bat.

I stopped, felt my heart jump. Then jump again.

"Oh, yeah," János said, "Mr. Weiler called the house."

My goddamm heart kicked in again, like it did when Millie's mom opened the door. I looked hard at my brother's face to see if I could read anything on it I didn't already know. The look in his eyes was familiar. He always sided with my parents.

János said he took the call himself. Actually, the old man took it, but it wasn't long before he handed the phone to János.

"What'd the old man say?"

"You know. *Entschuldigen Sie,* but I no speaka-de-Anglais. You know his hearing and his English are shot. But your Mr. Weiler, he was something else. Man, he raged over the phone like a mad dog. Said you were caught having sexual intercourse with his daughter. He's going to get you, man. If you ever, ever go within five blocks of his house again, he's going to bash your head in. Those were his exact words. Hey, let me ask you something right now," János said. "Did you have to do it in the dining room? I mean—"

"Shut up!"

"I did," János said. "Let me put it this way. You owe me one. The intercourse part? It got lost in the translation."

"Alright, what'd you say?"

"I told the old man it was a Hoover salesman who had the wrong number. But seriously, man. You're better off not messing around with her."

I was still in a daze. I didn't know what to say.

My brother was quick to tell me I was an asshole for doing what I did.

"What did I do? Make love?"

"Love, huh? On the dining room table. Okay."

"You don't understand."

He didn't.

I told him I didn't want to talk about it.

János did. And in the worst way. He wanted to know if I was caught with my bare ass out, or what? Was I able to stop? János was rabid. He said once intercourse got started, there was no stopping. There were studies at a university. About apes. A fucking ape got hit over the head with a hammer during the physical act of love, and he just kept on going. "The fucker just kept right on going. Man! Of course, maybe a baseball bat's a different story. Get it? Hey, what did her mother say exactly, word for word?"

"You're an asshole," I said.

"Yeah, I'm the asshole."

"You're an asshole and you don't even know it."

"She's a Jew, man!"

I decked him. I hit János so hard he crashed into the hedges. That wasn't enough. I pounced on him like a freaking ape. I kept hitting him and hitting him. I was getting the better of him. For once, I was getting the better of my older brother. All János could do was butt my chest with his head. My fists kept working. "Take that, you mother! And that!" János tried to shield himself by crossing his arms in front of him. My barrage of punches wouldn't let up. I heard my mother yowling above us, but I didn't stop. She'd taken off one of her shoes and was hitting my back with her high heels, but I didn't stop hitting my brother. I was a freaking ape, too. We were all freaking apes.

Suddenly I stopped.

I stopped because I suddenly felt sorry for Millie for hooking up with a bunch of freaking apes.

I tried calling her house several times that night and through the weekend—only to hang up when her father answered the phone. I felt weird. I wasn't worried about my ass so much as I was about Millie. If her old man was ready to bash my head in with a baseball bat, what was he going to do to her? Christ! Would he ship her off to another school? Just to keep her away from me? Her parents talked of Montreal once. Even Paris. Millie had applied to these schools around the time we broke up. When I was riding the train from one end of the line to the other writing those morbid poems about death.

With Monday came my first day in college. I was more anxious than excited. I felt hot and cold all day, like I had chills or a fever. I was anxious for Millie and anxious for myself. I wasn't gung-ho about Cleveland State, the very name of the school was depressing. I hadn't slept much the last couple of days, either, and it showed. My eyes burned, I was itching all over. There was a weird rash on my hands, elbows and chest.

I took an early bus to West Park Rapid station, tossed away a half-smoked cigarette when the train came. The book bag felt heavy as shit. I sat down by a bunch of empty seats. The last thing I needed was human contact. I opened my bag and took out my textbooks. Scientific German. Dog shit. I stuffed it back. A large overpriced Biology book with color pictures of the insides of frogs. Shit. My Physics and Calculus textbooks stared back at me like ogres. But the most frightening book of all was the thick medical book my father bought me as a graduation present. It was the same book doctors used to diagnose disease, my father said, and it was supposed to give me a jump start over my peers as a pre-Med student. I opened the book to a random page, read the symptoms and latched on to them.

Fatigue, lassitude, malaise. I didn't know what "lassitude" meant, but I knew I had it. That and an itchy rash all over my frigging body. I picked up *something* lying in the tall grass. Poison ivy would be too easy, it had to be something a lot more lethal. The old feeling was back. My father had bought me a book of torture that would last eleven years. And this was day one.

My first day as a college freshman turned out to be a total blur like I was on drugs or something. I dragged myself through my classes, then lugged my heavy ass bag back to the Rapid-Transit, antsy about getting home in case Millie called.

She didn't.

I realized I missed soccer practice. Shit. Practice was every day at four. Our first game was Saturday against Ohio State. I didn't want to screw up soccer. CSU had given me an athletic scholarship for the first semester. It was a pretty big deal. Pretty freaking big. Now I had to make something up to tell my coach. But maybe I wouldn't have to. The rash on my hands, arms and chest was blistering, itching like a mother. What the hell was it anyhow? Poison freaking sumac! I scratched the red blisters, went into the bathroom to look for something to put on them. Nothing in the medicine cabinet except a dead spider. Freaking house. I ran steaming hot water over them, they just itched more.

I couldn't believe Millie didn't call.

Before we got caught, she told me she was going to call as soon as she knew her phone and address at the Cleveland Institute of Art. But she didn't call. She didn't call Monday, she didn't call Tuesday or Wednesday. Come Thursday, my Scientific German prof called my name out in class. Was there a Mr. Art Nagy in the room?

It wasn't Millie, but a cop from the Fairview Park Police Department. He drove me to the station for questioning. They were responding to a complaint of statutory rape.

Hearing those words ran a shiver up my spine. I was nauseous. I felt bad about everything, especially Millie. She was just 17, and I was 18 when we started doing it. In the eyes of the law, she was a minor and I was an adult. I was old enough to think for myself. Old enough to know better.

Millie wasn't at the station. Nobody seemed to be there. A Sergeant Lang who was supposed to question me wasn't in yet. Not for a while. I spent a shitload of time trying to figure out all the stuff that went on in my life that lead up to all this. It would be a mouthful, that was for sure.

Sergeant Lang cleared his throat when he came in. He said he was sorry for having kept me waiting.

I was really floored by the Sergeant's first question: "What was Millie Weiler like?"

I didn't get it.

"With boys. What was she like with boys? Was she easy?"

I dug my nails into the armrest. I told the cop Millie wasn't like that. It was all my fault.

"Well," he said, smiling, "actually you're a pretty lucky dog. The girl just turned 18, but of course you knew that. I take it that was your first time. One helluva way to celebrate her birthday, right?"

I was not about to say anything to this asshole.

"Well, Mr. Weiler is pretty upset. I would be, too, if you know what I mean. You look like a smart kid. The smartest thing you could do for yourself right now is to stay away."

I nodded.

"One more thing. Millie wants you to stay away, too."

CHAPTER 6

On a Friday, a couple of weeks after my stint at the police station, I cut all my classes, grabbed one of my rarely worn sports coats and tidied myself up so I'd be taken seriously at the Cleveland Institute of Art. Hell or high water, I was hellbent on finding Millie.

The Art Institute, on the east side of Cleveland, was at most a 45-minute drive. Millie could've easily commuted, and when I first heard she was going to live there in a dorm, I chalked it off to that one word again. Status. Now there was another reason. Me. They had to keep her away from me. I guess living in the same city was too close for comfort: She would've had a nice drive taking the Shoreway and Liberty Boulevard, which snaked through a big-ass park leading to the Cleveland Art Museum. The Institute of Art was right next door. By car, it was a cinch, but by bus and train it was a pain. I knew from my three-year commute to Cathedral Latin. My old school and a couple of universities and Severance Hall, home of the Cleveland Orchestra, were all in the same area, a block or two from each other.

My old man once took the family to Severance Hall to hear Liszt, Wagner, and Berlioz. He bawled through a rendition of "Rákoczy's March." He was sensitive one minute, a raging lunatic the next. I wondered if my old man's crazy-ass temperament was genetic.

Thank God I didn't inherit his weak constitution. He was a smoker and a lunger, I was a smoker and a soccer player. When I forgot about dying of heart disease or some other dreaded illness, I considered myself to be in top shape. I ran wind sprints almost daily for the college soccer team. I was especially proud of my strong legs. Weight training and endless squat thrusts developed my calf muscles until they looked like I had bricks under the skin, and at nearly every free kick opportunity the team called on me to take the shot. My right leg was especially deadly.

If Mr. Weiler wanted to whack me with a baseball bat, just let him try. He would have to face my deadly right. Or left. Because the strength in my left was catching up with my right. Just let him try! Just try it, Mr. Weiler. And if you do anything weird to Millie, you're going to get your freaking head kicked in. My muscles contracted instinctively. I had freaking pistons for legs.

Choice thoughts on the long train ride. I had something on me in my book bag, something to give to Millie. It was a copy of the CSU *Cauldron*. The sports section carried a photo of me in action against Ohio State. The write up mentioned my name:

> *"Art Nagy, a freshman who plays right inside for the Vikings, booted his first goal on a hard, straight as an arrow shot into the far corner of the nets. The Buckeye goalie defending the goal made a desperate lunge for the ball but ended up sliding on his belly."*

Just try it, Mr. Weiler.

What if Millie really wanted me to stay away, too? I didn't want to think about it because then I'd feel this cold nausea in my chest and find myself on the verge of crying. I might even bawl, like my old man in Severence Hall. I didn't like that. I didn't like that at all. Sensitive one minute, a raging lunatic the next.

Once off the train, I had no patience for the connecting shuttle and walked instead to Euclid Avenue past the statue of Lajos Kossuth, a Hungarian patriot who came to America after the fall of the Hungarian War of Independence. Kossuth's Hussars even fought in the American Civil War on the Union side. Hungarians were known to be fierce warriors. Swift, reckless, especially in the counter-attack.

Just try it, Mr. Weiler.

Kossuth's statue had a large cardboard sign hanging from his neck: MAKE LOVE NOT WAR.

I picked up my pace.

The Art Institute's main building sat on East Boulevard across from the Cleveland Museum of Art. By mistake, I wandered into the Reinberger Galleries. The art pieces displayed there amazed me. One looked like a huge spitball made of old newspapers. Another was a tangle of rusty pipes titled *The Maze*.

I asked a girl wearing a torn T-shirt, paint-splattered jeans and combat boots if she knew where they would have a list of art students. I was looking for a Lyudmilla Weiler. Without looking up, she told me the Registrar would be my best bet.

I headed over to the administration offices in another building. The Registrar turned out to be a thin woman with graying hair and a scrubbed face. She said she was sorry, but she could not give out that kind of information. I nodded and walked off. I strolled over to the museum grounds and planted myself on a park bench across from the statue of Rodin's *The Thinker*. I was still within sight of her school. Maybe I'd be lucky enough to spot her. I had a few cigarettes left and a salami sandwich that smelled like moth balls. My old man got this industrial strength deodorizer for the fridge, stuff they use for urinals. It made our food smell like a freaking john. He was too cheap to toss it. Not that I was the least bit hungry.

After an hour, I got restless and walked up the museum steps, only to find out they were closed. I waited another hour, watching the swans in the lagoon, then started my long trek back. During soccer practice later that afternoon, I was so angry I injured a teammate in a brutal sliding tackle.

The coach was furious. "Come on, Art. There's no call for that."

The hot shower after practice made what was left of my stupid rash itch like hell. The first time my teammates saw the red blotches on my skin, they thought they looked pretty gross. "Stay away. Freaking leprosy, man!"

Another week went by without any sign from Millie. Then another. I had already flunked a few tests. I had no patience whatsoever reading about stuff like the "heterotroph hypothesis" in frigging biology. Scientific German was a pain in the ass. Bunching all those words together was stupid. They had this one word for the whole Theory of Relativity," something like "*Relativitatsteorie*." Dog shit.

I was hoping we'd be reading poetry in my English Composition class but all we talked about were topic sentences and thesis statements. Finally, we read a book that wasn't all that bad. *My Antonia*. The description of the Nebraska prairie reminded me of southern Hungary. Fields and fields of pale stalks rustling dryly in the wind. I wrote about it in my English class, and I was surprised when I saw a big red "A" on the cover of my blue book and the words "See me."

I went to see my instructor, Mrs. Knowles, who wore a pin on her dress in the shape of quote marks. Mrs. Knowles said she thought I had talent for writing and asked if I would like to meet with a Dr. Oszlányi, a Hungarian professor who was a writer and who also taught German Literature.

Dr. Oszlányi was nice enough to invite me to his home. The professor was a short elderly gentleman with wire-rimmed glasses and a pencil-thin mustache. He published in obscure Hungarian-American magazines.

Dr. Oszlányi showed me some samples of his articles. Most of them dealt with the evils of Communism. Dr. Oszlányi said, "Imagine, my asinine colleagues are flirting with Communism. They're nothing but armchair Communists with gilded anniversary editions of Marx on their coffee tables. Ash Can Oligarchy. The Aristocracy of the Proletariat. Do you understand any of this?"

I didn't but said I did. I told him I was at the Institute of Art and saw crushed ash cans mounted on a wall.

"Precisely," Dr. Oszlányi said. "Degenerate art."

Dr. Oszlányi's wife came in with a tray of fragrant espresso and poppy-seed rolls. She was beaming. She said my mother did her hair regularly at the beauty shop. She was one of my mother's satisfied customers. She asked me how I liked it at Cleveland State. Their daughter was away at Princeton but would be back for Thanksgiving. Maybe I could visit then?

Maybe.

Once his wife left the room, Dr. Oszlányi was anxious to get back to politics. He said his Department was unhappy with him because of his political views. In fact, he was under surveillance. The CIA was tapping his phone. He opened a desk drawer and pulled out a 3 by 5 index card, which he tossed on the desk. "Go ahead, pick it up and read it," he said.

The handwritten note on the card read: "*Dr. Oszlányi is under my professional care for the treatment of malignant hypertension. His mind, however, is not impaired.*" The last two words were under-scored in red. The note was signed by a Dr. Julius Vajda, M.D.

Another Hungarian nutcase, I thought.

"Now then," said Dr. Oszlányi, "what do you have to show me? Professor Knowles says she's pretty impressed with you."

I said I had these poems, but Dr. Oszlányi didn't give me a chance to show them.

"So, you think you're going to be a great poet. So, you suffer from delusions of grandeur. My advice to you, young man, is to keep a journal and save everything. Where do you work?"

"McDonald's. Part-time."

"I want you to write there, too. Write on paper napkins, receipts, any scrap of paper you can get your hands on. On matchbooks. Write on the wall, if you have to."

Saturday our college team traveled through the rolling Pennsylvania country side to play at Slippery Rock College. Most of the players were busy yapping, clowning. A few read, hunched over heavy textbooks. I could never read on the bus, I'd get nauseous if I tried. What I did was stare out the window at the passing red and orange hills and soft grass, thinking about Millie and me sledding down the hill, turning over and rolling into each other. Where was she? In a goddamm nunnery? You can't just fall off the face of the earth. Three weeks now and not one phone call or letter. Three weeks! I was so bummed out, soccer seemed like a chore. Here I was somewhere in freaking Pennsylvania, running around on a soccer field. I just didn't have the drive to pounce on the ball anymore. It was just another ball rolling on the grass. Coach pulled me out. CSU and Slippery Rock were tied at one goal apiece when there was a foul called in the penalty area. Coach called me off the bench to take the penalty kick.

It should've been a sure goal. But I wanted to kick the shit out of the ball so it tore off the freaking net.

I missed. The ball sailed over the bar by a mile. Shit. Should've taken the easy shot. Could've tapped the ball in with the side of my foot, but I had to go for the kill. We were still undefeated, and now we had one draw, thanks to me.

Things were not going all that well these days. The University's Early Warning System sent me a warning, putting me on notice that I was failing three of my classes, the pre-Med core, to be precise, Biology, Chemistry and Calculus. Art Nagy, M.D. never seemed more remote.

What was bothering me most about school was that it wasn't bothering me. I figured that sooner or later I'd be 1-A anyhow and the draft would get me. I would end up in the jungles of Vietnam, picking up dead GI's in a Chinook until I myself was a dead GI with a dog tag. I had a dog's life, why not a dog's death? Dog shit.

Gypsy tried cheering me up Sunday by dragging me to one of the Hungarian Hunters' soccer games. They were going to play the

Romanians and they were a couple of guys short. I told him about NCAA rules and losing eligibility and all that shit, but he wouldn't take a no. After a couple of beers in the basement of my uncle's bar and grill, he talked me into it. Gypsy was doing stunts with his half thumb to get a rise out of me. I wasn't much for a laugh. I'd egg him on about scoring, though. And I wasn't talking about soccer. When he held his half-thumb by his groin, I said, "Yeah, give that to Anna." I was talking about the barmaid upstairs. The very Anna who was my uncle's girlfriend.

"Wanna get me killed? Thanks, man. Thanks, Attila."

I grinned and reminded him my new name was "Art."

He wasn't thrilled about my Americanized name either. As you can probably guess, my old man hated it. He said it reminded him of his first taste of Royal Castle's birch beer. He expected real beer but what he got was the sickly-sweet taste of tooth paste. A real letdown. My uncle was ape over it. My new name that is. It was a shortened version of his, and he wanted me to grow up to be just like him—a bullshit artist.

Gypsy said: "What's wrong with Attila the Hunk?"

"Not *Hunk* but *Hunky*," I said. "That's what those ass-wipes at school called me, once they found out my real name. Attila the Hunky. *Art* is classier."

"Classier?" Gypsy laughed and adjusted the balls in his jock. "You mean homo. Is that your new identity?"

"Give me a break. It's short for Arthúr, man."

"Got it. But why your uncle's name? He's a homo. You told me yourself."

"That's why you have to score with his girlfriend. You should at least feel sorry for her. She's hard up, man."

"But she's old."

"Old is good. Older chicks have experience. She can break you in, man."

Gypsy laughed like a hyena but then got suddenly serious and said he was going to score with a bicycle kick. He was going to do a full axel or some shit in the air, then go into a bicycle kick.

"Score with Anna!" I said. It was an order.

"Why don't you?"

"I had," I lied. I knew it was the beer talking but I plowed on. "In the cooler."

Sundays when she didn't work the bar for my uncle, Anna came to the games and sat on a blanket. Rumor had it the entire team had gone through her. She was part-time barmaid, part-time waitress and my uncle's part-time girlfriend.

Gypsy's dark eyes lit up. "When?"

"Before I met Millie. You should've seen her. She was all made up. Cleavage all over the place. She and my uncle were stirring up shit over a bowl of soup. Anna was saying her customer's bitching his soup's cold. She pushed the freaking bowl across the counter, spilling half the shit. My uncle ladled out another bowl and shoved it in with his steaks. He waited till it was boiling before he said, "*Noomber thr-ree*," into the mike. Y'know, in his Dracula accent. Anna's hips come swinging through the door. He tossed the pot-holder at her. Let the shithead scald his kisser off. Then he takes his cigarette and flicks the ashes right into the freaking soup. Man!"

"Get to the cooler part, Art boy," Gypsy was getting antsy. His small hand thrust another beer at me.

"Yeah. I'm in the cooler stuffing peppers, right? Anna switches off the mike and comes into the cooler real soft-like, pretending she was looking for some milk or shit. My elbow and her nipple touch. Contact! One thing led to another, and before you know it I'm humping her on a sack of potatoes."

"Yeah. Sure," Gypsy said.

"Yeah, man. I could've been dog meat. You know how he runs around with a cleaver. The cooler's door is open a slit. My uncle is screaming: 'Hey, your soup's getting cold.' Anna walked out first and then I shuffled out with a couple of peppers. And then something came over me. I grabbed the mike and called Anna's number in my sexiest voice: "*Number three.*" My uncle lost it. The psycho threw the cleaver at me. Missed me by an inch. He told me not to touch the mike again. Ever."

"So you got fired."

"So I got fired. But I hit a home run. Now it's your turn. See if you can get to first base."

"You get to first base with Millie yet?

"She's not easy. Damn near inaccessible. I still don't know where the hell she is. Pisses me off, man. But you! You! This is your big chance. Don't blow it."

I kept needling Gypsy about getting his kisser ready. In no time at all, he was swiveling on his bar stool, on the make. Anna poured us Cokes. On the house. "Give 'em beer," someone said at the end of the bar. Max Alvis was at bat on the boob tube. The Indians were playing the Red Sox in Boston. Alvis tapped the side of his shoe with his bat.

"Leave them alone," Anna said. "These boys are athletes."

Now that was a laugh. I nudged Gypsy. "Talk to her but don't come on like one of the Beatles," I coached. "Do your Country-Western."

Too late. Eyes pressed shut, Gypsy was already bleating, "I wanna hold your hand."

"She hates that, I'm telling you."

The team's loudmouth scoring ace from Budapest by way of Chicago, nicknamed Chicago, sidled up next to us. "Watch this," he said. He called Anna over. In patchy English he asked, "You know Dave Clarkfive? I'm Dave Clarkfive." The stupid ass thought the Dave Clark Five was a one-man band. And this was Mr. Man who was going to show us how it was done just because he had ten or so years on us. Anna batted her eyelashes but it was not a come-on. It was more like, "Are you nuts?" Chicago quickly shifted gears to the upcoming game. He told Gypsy, who was to play defense, to keep his eyes on the wonder-boy of the Romanians. If he scored, Gypsy'd get his dick cut off, not just his thumb.

"There goes your bicycle kick," I said to Gypsy.

"Screw the bicycle kick," Chicago said.

Anna did the driving to the Valley where we played our games. Uncle Arthúr would get a ride with the other players. Chicago slid between me and Gypsy in the back seat of my uncle's black Cadillac Eldorado. My uncle hoped to get into the funeral business and thought that by buying a black Eldorado he'd get a head start.

In the front seat, sitting shotgun where Anna usually sat, was a bald guy in his thirties. He was subbing for one of the regulars. Squeezed into the backseat, me and Gypsy drew our knees together to avoid contact with Chicago. Chicago was trying to talk Gypsy into sticking his half-thumb up Anna's ass. "You have to introduce yourself somehow," Chicago said.

Anna took the corners nicely. When we came to a stop, the car rocked and everybody lurched forward and said, "Woe-hoe."

"Don't do that," Anna said to the rearview. She must've felt something. "Save your strength for the net," said Anna, grimacing into the rearview.

"Aye, aye, Captain," Chicago said, always hyper before a match. Then he turned his attention to the bald guy in the passenger seat. "I heard MTK beat Ferencváros in Budapest, is that right?"

The bald guy nodded without looking back. They continued talking about matches in Hungary and the Olympics in Tokyo last summer. How the Hungarians took the gold in soccer and water polo as expected—but not without a fight. In the water polo semi-finals against the Russians, a Russian player struck a Hungarian player and it lead to a melee and blood in the pool. "The Japs caught the whole thing with their underwater camera. It was wild, man. Clouds of blood all over the place. Fucking Russians," Chicago said.

My thoughts drifted to the upcoming game. I had enough beer and adrenaline in me to forget about Millie and fantasize about scoring the goal of the century. I would take an aerial pass from Gypsy, maybe in the first 10 minutes of play and go up for the bicycle kick myself. The ball would slam off the bar by the left corner. I would even shout, "Left corner!" before I went up for it. Like calling a pocket in billiards. "Make the easy shot, don't try to be spectacular," my coaches told me a hundred times. "A goal's a goal, goddammit. You don't get any more points for being flashy." You'd think I had learned my lesson against Slippery Rock when I blew a penalty kick—but no! For me, "spectacular" was the name of the game. Otherwise, what was the point? Even if I missed the goddamm ball, I'd be up there, high in the air, almost flying...

Everyone laughed. Chicago must've said something crazy again. Traffic was bumper to bumper down the cobbled incline to the field. Chicago said, "I never cared much for MTK, to tell you the truth. That's one club that's always been pink as far as I'm concerned."

I knew enough from Uncle Arthúr that by "pink" Chicago meant Communists or Jews. "My uncle says it's all a bunch of kikes," I heard myself volunteer. I had no idea why I said it. It just came out of my mouth.

Silence.

"You blew it this time, sport," Chicago said. "Jakab here is from Israel. He plays in the Jewish League."

Laughter.

"What I meant was—"

"It's alright. You blew it."

Yeah, I blew it and I was pissed. Game-time couldn't have come soon enough. But once the game got started, time just zipped by and by halftime we were already down by 2. Our opponents, the Romanian Rebels, had these black smudges painted under their eyes to keep down the glare or to make them look fierce. Instead of looking like war paint it looked like the cheap shit shoe polish that it was. Our once proud Hungarian flag, with its old Kossuth coat of arms dating back to the Revolution of 1848, served as one of the corner flags.

A typical Cleveland rain out of nowhere chased the fans under the trees. As insane as it was, I looked for Millie among the thin line of spectators. Anna was the only female among them. Someone gave her an umbrella. After the whistle, which signaled the start of the second half, Chicago tapped the ball to me. Our unspoken understanding was that I should pass it back to Chicago no matter what, but something came over me and I kept dribbling the ball in a mad dash toward the goal.

In an instant the Romanians were all over me. I lost the ball and my footing and found myself sprawled on my ass, muddy all the way to the jock. Frigging Romanians! Gotta get reckless. To hell with technique. I gave up wanting to fly through the air and score with the bicycle kick. I yelled to Gypsy to go in for the kill. "Gypsy!" I shouted, "Kamikaze all the way, man!"

The ball sailed toward me. I couldn't head it, but I made damn sure the Romanian next to me couldn't, either. With my spikes planted in the mud, I stuck out my ass and elbows in a mean shove. The Romanian came down off balance. Whistle. I raised my hand. I had to turn around so the referee could see my number. A yellow card.

On the next play the wonder-boy of the Romanians was dribbling between me and Gypsy. I wedged my right foot between the Romanian's ankles, causing the wonder-boy to fly headlong inside the penalty area.

Another whistle. Shit.

The Romanian was holding his knee in agony.

"He's faking it," I protested.

The Romanian player gritted his teeth. I stomped my boot near his head and splattered mud in his eyes. Take that, you mother!

I was hit from behind, lost my breath and doubled over.

Gypsy butted in and got sucker punched in the mouth. Spectators from the sidelines rushed in with sticks, soda bottles, baseball bats. A flurry of kicks kept me from crawling an inch. Where I wasn't smarting, I felt numb. Gypsy tore through the mob holding the Hungarian flag like a spear. I was trying to slither along on my belly when something blunt caught the side of my head. The last thing I saw was Gypsy, his face a spider of blood streaks.

Me and Gypsy found ourselves propped against the back of my Uncle Arthúr's black Eldorado. A home-made bumper sticker in Hungarian read: *Undertakers Do It Last.* At least I thought it was in Hungarian. My head was feeling really crappy. Like it wasn't screwed on right. The door on the driver's side looked like it was bashed in with a sledgehammer. All four tires flat. Anna was crying. My uncle snapped several Polaroids of "injuries sustained." The first was of Gypsy and me, the other a close-up of Gypsy showing the split lip where he was sucker punched. It looked like an inverted dark red V. His gums glistened weirdly. His kisser was done for. "It'll be as good as new," Uncle Arthúr told Gypsy. "A few stitches. Those bastard Romanians are in for it once the league sees the grievance report."

"Yeah, you gave it to him good," someone quipped. "That shit-eating ref didn't know what hit him."

"Quiet. The kid only opened his thigh. Screw the Ref!" said Uncle Arthúr. "We'll get 'em."

I felt queasy and waited for the feeling to go away. "How's the head feel?" A thread of saliva floated from my chin. I wiped myself with the sleeve of my jersey.

"We better get him to a hospital," someone who sounded a lot like my old man said. I was surprised I didn't recognize the woman helping me to a car.

"What's your name?" the doctor asked.

I didn't know. Not even a clue.

"Where do you live?"

A voice in the back of my head tried answering the freaking questions but, for some weird reason, nothing came out of my mouth. I knew my name began with the letter *A* but I had no idea what came after.

"Don't you remember your name?"

I didn't. I didn't know who I was or where I was, but I had a pretty good idea where I lived. "1 Párisi Street," I said. Then I heard a groan.

The doctor said, "Your father's here. He says that's your god-mother's address in Hungary. Where you lived eight years ago. Know where you live now?"

The man who said he was my father said in Hungarian that it was time I dropped the tough guy act and told the good doctor where we lived.

"1 Párisi Street. Budapest. Why? What happened?" I thought I had been shot. I was sure of it. I was shot in the head during the Hungarian Revolution. I thought I was going to get sick to my stomach.

But they kept asking me questions, like how old I was, and what the date was and all that. I figured as long as I kept my mouth shut I wouldn't throw up. I wanted to tell them I am 9 years old and it's 1956. October 23, 1956. We were being shot at. I was at the demonstrations on Petőfi Square in Budapest. I remember a man on a platform reciting "Rise Up, Magyars":

> *Rise up, Magyars! Your country calls!*
> *The time is here! It's now or never!*
> *Shall we be free or slaves forever?*

"FREE!" the crowd cheers. More and more people fill the square. There must be thousands. People are holding posters and flags. Students arm in arm from the nearby university, workers from the factories, wearing their work clothes and berets. I climb a lamp post so I could see. People everywhere. Hungarian flags, many with a hole where the red star is supposed to be. They're shouting: *Ruszkik haza!* Russians Go Home! A red flag goes up in flames. We hear there is another demonstration at Heroes Square where they are going to pull down the statue of Joseph Stalin.

My mother and me take the subway to the square. Every station is a mass of people. It's worse than after the soccer game when Hungary beat England 7 to 1. Something tells me there will be no homework due in the morning, or the morning after that.

Heroes Square is overflowing with a cheering mob. A truck's headlights lights up Joseph Stalin's metal knees. There is a steel noose around his neck. The truck's engine whines. The metal knees creak then buckle. The great father and liberator is buckling at the knees. The metal rips just under the knee, leaving a pair of hollow boots. As they drag his trunk on the cobblestone, there are sparks each time it hits the trolley tracks. A woman spits. Shouting. Screams. Someone in the crowd says AVO men, the secret police, are stashing guns into the city sewers. "Flush them out!" the crowd shouts. "Flush out the rats!"

Now it's my godmother who grabs my arm and pulls me alongside her. Where is my mother? We make our way through the crowd back to the subway. But there are so many people by the entrance, we can't take the subway back. We have to walk. Then we hear gunfire. The crowd is going crazy. I smell gasoline. More and more people are yelling, "Flush out the rats!"

My godmother is looking for a place to hide. We run through an alley to a church. The heavy doors creak open. The stained glass windows and the altar are dark. She takes me over to the statue of the Virgin Mary. I ask her why the statue's nose is broken off like that. She takes a deep breath and says, "The last war." I nod as if I know. I don't want to ask any stupid questions.

I let go of her hand and head back to the big doors. That's when I realize it's Millie that I left waiting at the altar. I know it's dumb but I open the door. That's when the shooting starts. RAT-TAT-TAT. Like that! Bullets fly everywhere. She screams. The next thing I know, I am lying on the cold floor. She's on top of me, her arms hugging me so tight I can't breathe. "*Ahhhhh—ttila!*" I hear her scream my name.

The doctor told me to open my mouth as wide as I could and to make the "*A*" sound as he looked in my throat. The "*A*" sound. The first letter of my name. I was making the "*A*" sound continuously now.

"*Ahhhhh—ttila,*" I blurted out. It sounded more like gagging.

"Thank God!" my father said.

"Attila. Attila Nagy. My name is Attila Nagy."

"Finally. Finally," my father said. "You've come to your senses.

"What happened?"

"You've got a head injury," the doctor said.

"I'm 9 years old," I said. "We're on No-Man's Land." I felt my head where it hurt. My ear was the size of a cauliflower. "On No-Man's Land. I got hit on No-Man's Land."

My father shook his head violently. "On the soccer field, for Chrissake. Quit playing games."

A woman with dark frizzy hair tried to give me a hug. I never heard of a nurse doing that. Nurses don't give hugs out of the blue. She looked hurt when I shrugged her off. "Don't you know who I am?" she asked.

"No."

"Oh my God! He doesn't recognize me! I'm your mother." She came in for a hug again.

"No you're not!" I was angry and getting angrier. "I never saw you before in my life. You're not my mother! Get away from me!"

CHAPTER 7

The doctor came in to examine my head again and ask more questions. I still didn't have the right answers. My head hurt like hell right by the spot where I thought I got shot. I was so strung out I thought I was losing it. He told me to give it time. I had amnesia. But it was only temporary and slowly things would come back. I hoped so because my old man and that woman were sure mad when they left here.

My father was back, in the evening, by himself. I suppose he thought he could speed things up by telling me about me. He probably thought he could jar loose a memory or two. First of all, he told me I was 18 and not 9. That was a surprise. Then he told me I didn't have a bullet hole in my head. That was a little hard to believe since my head was covered with bandages. He told me that when I was 9, during our escape, a bullet grazed me, but it didn't happen in a church. It was on a truck. When I kept asking me where my mother was, he said she was here, but I didn't recognize her. "It's your head," my father said. "The concussion. You're all confused. You have your mother confused with your godmother. Don't tell me you don't remember your Aunt Piroshka. She's your godmother. You lived with her a long time. I told your mother it was a bad idea. I just knew it. That sooner or later it would come to this. Now you can't even recognize her. Your poor mother."

So now I had two mothers, was that it? And a brother named János. I really must've gotten creamed. My brain was fuzzy as all get-out. But the feeling that I missed somebody who was soft and who loved me wouldn't go away. It wasn't my mother or my aunt. It was someone else. Someone in the Church of Our Lady in Montreal or Paris. Whoever she was, I missed her. She made my chest hurt like hell. My father and the doctor said everything would come back, starting with more recent memory, like the soccer game. But it didn't make any sense. The more shit I remembered, the crummier I felt. I felt bad for Gypsy for trying to set him up with my uncle's girlfriend. Telling him to go kamikaze so we get the shit beat out of us.

My old man wanted to know more about the soccer game. He wanted to know who it was that whacked me like that. He said he had no doubt it was intentional.

"What?"

"Did you get a good look at him? He was bald, wasn't he?"

"Oh, Jakab. You mean Jakab. No, No. He's on *our* team for crying out loud. He's Hungarian."

"Sure he is. With a name like Jakab *Rosenberg*?" my father said, looking around. "He really scrambled that brain of yours, didn't he? You think the Jewish League is just another league like your Lake Erie League? You have a lot to learn, boy! Somehow they got hold of our number. We get these calls and click, they hang up. Now we're going to have to get another unlisted number!"

Oh God, I thought. Not again. I didn't want to hear this. I pretended to doze off. My old man got tired of watching me and left for the lobby and a smoke.

The next day, I got a roommate. Marvin, the kid in the next bed, was from New York somewhere and pronounced his name Mah-vin. I must've been talking in my sleep because his nurse told him I had a concussion and amnesia and sometimes patients like me had vivid dreams. Mah-vin himself was recovering from a hernia operation.

Gypsy, his head wrapped in gauze like a mummy, had himself wheeled to my semi-private room. I was glad to see a familiar face. His nurse said she'd wheel him back to the ward down the hall when he was done. All the players had insurance, Gypsy didn't. I asked Mah-vin to repeat in front of Gypsy what his operation was for.

"I shat too hard," Mah-vin said. "You know, on the toilet."

Gypsy shook his head. "I didn't get it at first, either," I said. "*Shat* is past tense for *shit.*"

Gypsy didn't laugh.

Lowering my voice, I told Gypsy my father was getting paranoid again. "He thinks Jakab's the one who clobbered me. He told me once that when he used to be a big-time judge before the war, he had these three Commies strung up. Jews. One of them was a Jakab Rosenberg. Yeah, the same name. Crazy, huh? My stupid old man thinks Jakab is the man's son. Hell-bent on revenge. Whew!…Hey, is Jakab's last name Rosenberg or Rose?" I asked Gypsy. "Gypsy? Isn't Jakab's last name Rose? My head isn't screwed on right, man." I looked at Mah-vin for a reaction but didn't get any. He was busy watching a special about the Beatles. Gypsy didn't say anything, either.

I started to feel clammy so I shut my trap. Gypsy worked his wheelchair closer to my bed and I thought for sure my buddy would say something to crack us up. "Hey, you're not saying anything, man," I said to Gypsy. "Hey, Gypsy, I said, "Would you give Millie a call? She won't return my calls."

"He can't talk," Mah-vin said, his eyes still glued on the flickering screen. "Can't you see his jaw is wired?"

I made an effort to prop myself on the pillow when the muscle that connects my stomach and chest gave suddenly. My head fell back and I felt weaker for trying to sit up. Sweat burst out coldly all over my body.

I drifted in and out of sleep all day and most of the night. I was really out of it, really weirded out. Maybe it was the pain pills. I had like these really strange flashbacks. I'm always four years old or close to it. My Uncle Arthúr is standing in his underwear painting a portrait of my Aunt Piroshka. He's working on getting the fingers holding the cigarette just right. The next thing I know she stops posing and pats her lap. That's when I notice I'm naked. "Attila, Attila," she says while my uncle fools with his paintbrush. "Come to Auntie." Ashes from her cigarette fall into the folds of her striped bathrobe. I sit on her lap. Her cigarette is making my eyes sting. "Okay," she says, "roll over." She is biting my butt. Little puppy bites. "I'm going to eat you! Yes. I'm going to eat you!" She's breathless between kisses. Then she stops and says to her husband: "Your turn. And no skimping, you hear! This boy is going to be a great man one day and you'll be lucky to have kissed his ass."

My uncle laughs. My aunt goes back to work on my bottom, purring, making motor sounds with her lips. I squeal. "See, he likes it more than I do. You love it don't you? I'm his godmother, I should know." It's bedtime, but it's not dark outside. Now Uncle Arthúr is wearing nothing but a pajama top. My godmother tells me she loves me more than my mother. "Let your uncle give you a kiss. He loves you more than your father." I start to cry because I don't want to go to bed. They give me a spoonful of sugar. My godmother tells me my favorite bedtime stories about Attila the Hun and the White Stag. I cry myself to sleep anyway, only to wake up in the middle of the night between my godmother and godfather. The sheet is cool and sticky by my bottom.

Then I see myself again at age nine. There's shooting in the streets. I'm supposed to stay away from the windows. Just yesterday we almost got shot in this old church. My godmother is taking nervous puffs from her cigarette. She is holding a large wad of American dollars in her hand. "When your uncle comes home tonight," she says. "Are you listening, darling? When he comes in tonight, we'll have to tell him someone broke into the apartment and threatened me with a pair of scissors. For this." She weighs the money in her hand. "I'm giving it to your mother." She stuffs the bills into an ivory horn among her knick-knacks. She kisses me, leaving lipstick on my face. She says she knew I would be marvelous. The ivory horn is going to be mine one day. It goes all the way back to ancient Hungarian mythology. The Legend of the White Stag. "It's settled," she says. "I'm not letting you go back to her. You're mine, and that's that." It's dark now and she's drawing me a bath. I ease myself into the hot water when the doorbell rings. "It's him," she whispers and hurries out the door. I let my neck rest against the tub. Then I hear Uncle Arthúr shouting, "I don't believe you."

"Please," my aunt pleads with him.

"Don't *please* me."

"Stop your barking."

"Shut up. Where is he?"

It's quiet again, except for the distant sound of gunfire. I wait for a door to slam, but nothing. I close my eyes, and when I open them again, I see the door ajar and my uncle looking at me, without saying anything. This time he has nothing on. The hot water is draining me. My uncle closes the door and lowers his voice, but they continue fighting. My uncle tells my aunt not to bother, that her goddamm family is going to suck them dry. "But we get Attila," my aunt says. "He's not going to America with them. My sister said I could keep him."

I'm motionless in what is now cold water. For a long time nothing is said. They must've forgotten about me. I get out of the tub and open the door a slit. The drawing room is dark. Lights flicker from Párisi Street. My godmother tip-toes toward the bedroom. My uncle follows her.

When she comes to wake me in the morning, she whips off my cover. I feel bad I may have wet their satin sheets, but she doesn't worry about that. She looks at me. She says it's not healthy to sleep in. It could lead to catalepsy. She wants to show me how to exercise mornings. "Ever watch a cat? How they stretch? Watch me." She goes through a series of stretches and groans, watching me, saying things like, "This is heavenly," and "Doesn't it feel good?" Then she turns into this big, gray cat.

At breakfast, my uncle insists my aunt's crepes are the best in the world. He tells me they seldom eat out because even the better coffeehouses, like the ritzy Gerbeaud, can't compete with the artistry of his wife's pastries. He has no idea how she does it. Of course they can't go out now even if they want to because, he says, it seems there's a revolution going on. He winks at my aunt. "Flattery will get you everywhere," my aunt says.

"Come here," my uncle says. She sits on Uncle Arthúr's lap. They both look at me.

"You don't want to go to America, do you?" my godmother says. "You're staying put with us. That's all there's to it. Your mother's all for it."

My uncle stops chewing and kisses her with a loud smack. Now I see that it's not my aunt at all, but Millie who is sitting on my uncle's lap. She gets off his lap, comes over and touches me. My uncle fades out like a fade-out in a movie.

I realize I'm in a hospital. It's dark except for the red EXIT sign. I feel very tense. Instead of touching my horn, I'm touching myself. That's when the night nurse shows up with a blood pressure gauge to take my vitals. I pretend I'm asleep but my heart is pounding. She puts the cuff on my arm and pumps it up until it hurts. There's a slow hissing noise as she lets the air out. "Mother of God!" she says out loud. She takes another reading, this time on my other arm. After fifteen minutes or so, she comes back and takes my blood pressure again.

In the morning, the nurse wheeled in an EKG machine to my bed and hooked me up. She ran out a strip, glanced at it and rushed out of the room. In minutes she was back with the doctor who had the EKG strip in his hand. The doctor asked me if I had any history of heart disease. I told him my mother and this Hungarian doctor in the village thought I needed an operation, but I didn't know for sure. Something about bad valves and an enlarged heart. The thing is, I told him, I've been playing soccer all this time. Even lettered in soccer. How could I play soccer with a bad heart?

The doctor ignored me. He was mesmerized by the spiking waves of my EKG. "Well, it doesn't look that bad. You have paroxysmal atrial tachycardia. It's not dangerous, but your parents ought to have it checked out by a specialist? Otherwise, everything is OK. You're making great progress. The swelling on the side of your head has gone down nicely." Before he left, he turned off the lights and checked my pupils with a pen light.

Mah-vin was out of the room for some tests. It was just me and the red EXIT sign. An hour went by, maybe two. I tried to sleep some but couldn't. The thing is, I wasn't feeling any better. Now I was worried about the freaking diagnosis. I wouldn't be able to pronounce the word if they put a Luger to my head. I took three years of Latin, but this gobbledygook shit was for real. Now what? Now I had a huge pain in my chest. Like someone was sitting on me. My skin felt flushed, my pulse raced. I was breathless, and I thought I was going to die. It wasn't long before tears streamed down my face. I felt a handkerchief wiping away the tears. I opened my eyes.

She said she was my mother.

"No you're not," I said, my breath quivering.

"Don't play with me like that," she said.

"I'm not playing," I said. I blew my nose, and what came out of my mouth afterwards sounded nasal and stupid. "If you're my mother, how come I still miss you? Tell me that."

"You're shaken up, son. Here, I brought you some cake. *Dobosh Torta*. Your favorite."

I broke down. Okay, she probably was my mother. But I was still angry. "You weren't with me in the church when they shot at us, were you? Or on the truck? Why weren't you in the car following us? It was just stupid old Uncle Arthúr!"

"But I'm here now," she said.

"I don't know you," I said.

"Who's there when you're sick, son? When your heart is ailing you? It's me, your mother."

"Why didn't you come with us?"

"I was too afraid for you. You were having heart palpitations every night. Every night! I couldn't live with myself if something happened to you. I just couldn't do it. That's the kind of mother I am. And when you and your father left us, your brother and I, we missed you so much, we followed right along. Not on the same day, but…we did find each other in Salzburg, didn't we?"

"The Red Cross found you."

She sighed. When she didn't get the last word in, she sighed. She was my mother alright.

My father said my mother was really worried about me. She wanted to take me to a specialist to make sure everything was okay. The doctor scared her.

"My heart?" I asked.

She nodded gravely.

I knew it.

The following day I was already home. I was told to avoid bright lights, flickering television, loud noises and excitement. In a week I should be all better. The first thing I planned to do was to look for Millie again. Where was she? Every time I thought of her my chest hurt.

One night my mother complained to my uncle about my heart. She told him it was probably soccer that had given me an enlarged heart. Maybe I shouldn't play. My uncle pulled me close to him so my chest was snug against his ear. I could see the pores of his skin and the two hairs on his nose. He held me tight while he listened to my heart. I felt it beating fiercely in my chest. After a full minute, my Uncle Arthúr pronounced: "Strong as a bull. Now get out of here."

I overheard them talking in the kitchen. My uncle told my mother that all athletes had enlarged hearts because they were stronger than normal hearts. Something else must be the matter. He was wondering what happened to my tough guy act. My mother said she was hoping I wasn't having a nervous breakdown. There was no mental illness on her side of the family. If it wasn't the heart, what else could it be? My uncle said he wouldn't worry about it. He was more concerned about my father's lung. I was worried about my father, too. He was losing weight and was thin as a scarecrow as opposed to my uncle who had thick forearms like a butcher, with sausages for fingers. When my father wasn't around, he liked to bug my mother about my old man's health. How could she go to bed with a lunger? The phlegm. The mucus.

The next day I went outside to kick the ball around in the driveway. I was kicking the ball pretty hard. By evening I felt lousy. My skin was hot, I had a pain in my chest, and I had trouble catching my breath. My mother had to come home early. My father was already at home pacing. I was sitting up in my bed with my hand on my chest. My mother put her hand on my chest and said, "It's racing alright."

"It's the soccer," my father said. "He can't just play like the others. He has to overdo it."

"I didn't overdo it." I said. "I was just kicking the ball around in the driveway. I have to stay in shape to keep my scholarship."

My mother sent me to the couch with a cold compress. I held the freaking thing to my chest while the two of them stayed in the kitchen doing their usual hush-hush shit. My father came back into the family room to tell me that soccer was over and done with, once and for all. He walked back to the kitchen and they whispered some more. They weren't talking about me at all, but fighting about Uncle Arthúr. Uncle Arthúr was making more money than my father. Uncle Arthúr was about to start his own business. ("Where did that shyster get all that money is what I'd like to know? A Swiss bank account or what?" my father hissed.) Finally, I heard my mother sigh, then the phone being dialed. My mother must've talked my father into calling the doctor.

Dr. Losonczy was a friend of the family. Of course, Dr. Losonczy was Hungarian. His office was on the fourth floor of a brownstone in the crummiest section of Cleveland's West Side. His building had no elevators, and the only way to get to him was by climbing a zillion steps. I had no great confidence in old Dr. Losonczy, and I made it known to my parents. I asked them about getting a specialist, like they said in the hospital. Dr. Losonczy was good for tetanus shots, even if he still boiled his needles, but the heart...?

"Now, what other doctor would come at the drop of a hat?" my mother said.

"And what other doctor has the distinction of being in a famous publication called *Who's Who Who's Not a Jew?*"

An hour went by, then two. The doctor must've left his house. There was no answer at his number. Then, finally, my father spotted his car. Dr. Losonczy had been going up and down our street for a quarter of an hour.

The doctor was led into the house, given a shot glass of *pálinka*. He followed it with a sigh and a piece of bread to counteract, he said, "whatever the liquor was unwittingly doing to my throat. A side effect well worth its therapeutic value." They talked about Adolf Eichmann's trial and execution, the political situation around the world, and what János Kádár's offer of amnesty could mean since the Stalin-type personality cult was now out of favor with the old boys on the Politburo—before Dr. Losonczy strolled into the room to ask me what was wrong.

I took the wet cloth from my chest and pointed to where it hurt, like a stupid little 9-year-old. If only they knew that up until a month ago I had a pretty active sex life—as a married man!

"So, you think it's the old ticker, eh?"

I thought that instead of "ticker" the doctor should be using words like "cardia" and "myocardium." The doctor said the old ticker was not on the left side but in the middle of the chest. He had a patient a while back who tried to kill himself by shooting himself on the left side where he thought his heart would be. He missed. By a long shot. Beginning fencers often make the same mistake, he said, and lunge in that direction. "Of course it would be good enough for match-point but in life hardly fatal."

My father grunted. All this meant they called the doctor for nothing. I spoke up saying I had been having attacks of pain and palpitations. Tachycardia.

"And you'd been reading books you shouldn't be reading," the doctor said. He listened to my chest for another thirty seconds, then said: "There's nothing here that a little rest won't cure."

The three of them strolled back into the kitchen. I heard Dr. Losonczy tell them that I had an enlarged heart and I was to abstain from vigorous exercise. My heart sank, hearing these words. Poor Millie bailed out just in time. She must've sensed defective goods. This meant it was the end of everything. I'd spend the rest of my life under house arrest. Shit, man! I wondered if my father and the doctor conspired against me. I strained my neck to listen, but could only make out a word or two. Dr. Losonczy was requesting another piece of bread to follow the *pálinka*.

I heard them laughing in the driveway. They kept talking in the driveway. My mother brought up my father's asthma attacks again, saying she didn't like him smoking and she didn't like him driving, especially at night. Then they put Dr. Losonczy in his car. He must've rolled down the window, because they kept on talking.

Eventually, I talked them into taking me to see an American cardiologist, a Dr. Hellerstein at University Hospitals.

My father fidgeted in the waiting room. Now and then he'd leave for a cigarette. He made no bones about being embarrassed for his son. By the time we got to the doctor's, I worked myself into a panic and was trembling. I said the room was too cold, the air conditioning too high. My father grunted. To make matters worse, I pulled out a rosary with some tissue when I reached into my pocket. When my father saw the rosary he raised an eyebrow and shook his head slowly. Pathetic.

Dr. Hellerstein told us there was nothing physically wrong with my heart. The EKG was normal. The doctor at Fairview Hospital overreacted. Paroxysmal Atrial Tachycardia (I had the ER doctor write down the words) was just a fancy word for rapid heart beat. Just adrenaline. I was probably nervous, he said. My heart rate was a tad fast, but nothing to worry about. Dr. Hellerstein asked me if anything was bothering me. Was I afraid of anything? Did I ever get angry and not know why? Was I under a lot of pressure?

I answered "no" to all these questions. Once my ticker got a clean bill of health, I lost interest. My father looked like he could use another cigarette.

"Are you nervous?" the doctor asked me.

"No."

He smiled: "Well, your fingers are drumming on my desk."

My hand froze. I may have turned red.

The doctor told me my problem may be too much adrenaline. Not unusual for adolescence. Was I under some emotional stress?

Nothing I could tell them about. I couldn't think of anything, other than my heart. And now that it was alright, everything was alright. I shook my head no.

"Just try to relax. Your heart is fine."

Still worried, I asked the doctor about soccer. Could I play with an enlarged heart?

"You don't have an enlarged heart, Attila. Who told you that? Soccer's good for your heart. Any vigorous activity."

I translated all this to my father, who bowed several times and said, "*Danke Schön*," but on our way home he yelled his head off: "You made quite a scene in the waiting room. Were you trying to impress this Jewish doctor with the rosary? Creeping Jesus! Maybe you are 9 instead of 18. When are you going to act your age? When are you going to get it into your head that it's all in your head. *Az agybaj nagybaj*," he said ominously. The Hungarian words meant "A mental case is a basket-case." It was one of my father's favorite sayings, and in Hungarian it even rhymed.

CHAPTER 8

I felt better once I got the hell out of the house. I headed straight for Gypsy's basement digs in the Projects, these ugly-as-shit concrete high rises around the Diamond Salt Company on the banks of the Cuyahoga River. The salt looked like a mountain range of dirty snow. A rusty, old barge was anchored there forever.

Gypsy was sunk into a bean bag, smoking a Camel. A red scar ran from his nose to his lip and chin. A tray of half-eaten French fries, cold and lardy, lay on a dish on the floor. Gypsy stabbed his cigarette into a mound of darkened ketchup when I came in. His record player was on full blast. I waited for "Twist and Shout" to spin out.

"Sorry about your jaw, man. I heard about the hospital bill."

Gypsy looked at me as if I said something funny, sprang up, put the needle back on "Twist and Shout." When it came to the part where the Beatles whine "*Oooh*," Gypsy sang along, "*Oooh, shake it a baby.*"

We didn't hear Gypsy's older brother come down the steps. He had on his boxing gloves and he started jabbing at the air, sparring with me, pulling punches, talking between breaths. "What you think of that screwed-up team, huh? I told him to quit a long time ago. He's stupid. You're stupid, man!"

"They're assholes," I said.

"Yeah?? Does that include your Uncle Arthúr?" Gypsy's brother said tauntingly. "See the Caddy lately? Freaking spanking new. No insurance problems there, huh? Goddammit." Then he turned to Gypsy. "Aren't you even pissed off? What the hell's the matter with you?"

Gypsy ran his half-thumb by his forehead, as if he'd forgotten something. Then he said he needed to cut the grass and made a bee-line for the stairs. I looked though the smudge of a basement window. It didn't look like the raggedy salt and pepper grass needed any cutting, but it was Gypsy's part-time job. Anything to help with the rent.

"Aw, shit," his brother said, yelling after him.

I stood around with my hands in my pockets.

Outside the basement window, a line of stiff T-shirts hung from a line wire. Gypsy's rusty lawnmower rolled by. His brother was behind him, fuming, yelling at him.

I leafed through Gypsy's home-study chemistry book. The letters in the book were huge EASY EYE, the pages splattered with colored pictures, not a single formula anywhere. It was watered-down chemistry without math. Inside the back cover ran a pencil-written poem:

The Chemist
I live among sweet vapors,
Slim tubes and glasses,
And would rather die among these
Than change places with the Párisi King.

Signed "*The Gypsy King.*" The poor sucker couldn't even plagiarize right, despite the bold signature. I was sure it should've been Persian King instead of Párisi King. Párisi Street was the name of my aunt's street in Budapest. Gypsy's been hanging around me too long.

The test-tube rack still hung on the wall next to his skates. The colored water had long evaporated, and they were just tubes of colored glass. The light from the basement window made the reds and blues look like stained glass in some church in the old country. With the changing light outside, the colored bars moved in streams along the wall. Different hues of blue. It was weird.

I spotted the telephone on the wall.

I dialed Millie's home number. A strange, far away ring on the other end, maybe five times. Finally someone picked up the phone. My heart was in my throat. "Millie?"

"This is her mother. Millie's in Paris. Who is this?"

The muscles in my jaw froze.

I slammed the receiver and ran up the steps, taking them two at a time. In a flash I was outside the door and in the parking lot. That's when I spotted Chicago.

Chicago was supposed to pick me up at Gypsy's, to go to an emergency meeting of the Lake Erie Soccer League. Chicago was drumming his fingers against the dashboard. The rusty, old barge was still there, looming above the Projects.

"Whatsamatter?" Chicago asked. "You're face is beet red."

I said I was sparring with Gypsy's brother. Chicago said "groovy," and looked at his watch.

We climbed into his VW Bug. "How's the kid doing?" Chicago asked, tapping my knee as he shifted into gear.

I told him.

Chicago made a sour face. "The old man plans to dump him, you know."

I didn't get it. How could my uncle want to dump Gypsy when he knew Gypsy didn't have insurance?

Chicago shrugged and said let's wait and see what the league's head honchos are up to.

I still didn't get it. I couldn't think straight. I couldn't believe Millie was in Paris. Maybe her mother recognized my voice and made it up just so I give up and get lost. I had no intentions of giving up, but I didn't know what to do. The last thing I wanted to do was to go to a stupid Lake Erie Soccer League meeting in the First Ukrainian Church basement.

When he saw me and Chicago come in, Uncle Arthúr raised both eyebrows as a greeting. Next to him, Anna sipped ginger ale by the stand-up bar, the center of attraction in a basement that was more like an auditorium. Only about half of the hundred or so chairs were taken, but before long the joint was crawling with people. Old paper streamers hung limply from the ceiling. Red crepe paper covered the long table on the stage.

All the chairs were stenciled with *Bodnár & Sons Funeral Parlor*. This was the funeral parlor my Uncle Arthúr wanted to buy into. Yeah, he was a real piece of work, this uncle of mine. Had a finger in every pie, as they say. One time he was forging paintings which he tried peddling on the black market in Hungary, but they were so crappy there were no takers. He told my father he liked Impressionism because it required less paint. Paint was expensive under Communism. They were always running low on red. Then rumors hit he was a secret agent or double agent or some crazy shit like that. It must've been a step down for him here in America where he was mismanaging an ethnic soccer team in a basement. And now he was an undertaker's understudy.

Chicago looked around, said he guessed we missed the party, then gulped down three quick shots of whiskey. Soon, he was on his way to the men's room to throw up. "Someone should see that he's okay," Uncle Arthúr said. I started after Chicago.

"No, you stay," my uncle said. He handed me a piece of paper. "Here, you want to look this over." It was the grievance report. As I started to read it, Anna handed me a bottle of Budweiser.

> *The Hungarian Hunters of the Lake Erie League hereby protest actions by the Romanian Soccer Club that have ensued following the match of Sunday, 9 October, in which several members of the Hungarian squad were injured, two requiring hospitalization (see photo, Figures A and B).*

I flipped the paper over for a list of counter grievances submitted by the Romanians:

> ...*Gross misconduct on the part of the Hungarian spectators. 3. Rushing onto the playing field with an assortment of weapons. 4. Unprovoked attack by Hungarian player No. 6 who stabbed Referee Andrej Marinc with a flagpole (copy attached for Referees' Association). 5. Slashing the tires of Andrej Marinc's motor vehicle. 6. Abusive language on the part of...*

"Pretty bad," I said to Uncle Arthúr.

He nodded, pulled out a cigarette from a pack of Luckies, coughed until he was red in the face. "There is a way out. Maybe. Listen." He turned to me earnestly. "We talked about it, the players and me. There's only one way to save the team on this. But it has to be written up and presented today. In English. That's where you come in. If we tell the league that as a team we have taken action internally to punish ourselves and to prevent future occurrences of this type, the league might bite on it. What we need to tell them is that the Hungarian Hunters suspended player No. 6 for unsportsmanlike conduct during and in the aftermath of the October 9 contest. Even though injuries..."

I quit listening.

"What's the matter?"

I said nothing.

My uncle massaged his jaw. His dentures glistened weirdly. "You were a pretty loose cannon yourself. What was that all about? It could've been you, pal. Okey-doke?"

I started scribbling what he wanted translated. "How long will Gypsy be suspended?" I asked.

"A season or two."

"Is anyone going to be suspended from the other team? The Romanians? Because Gypsy put a lot of work—" I broke off. Chicago squeezed between us and ordered another whiskey. I felt my anger rising. "Chicago said you're trying to dump him because he's a Gypsy."

"Chicago has a run-on mouth on the field and off the field," my uncle snapped. "If only he could run as fast as he talks." Uncle Arthúr was saying Chicago was a word shitter.

Chicago grabbed me and put me in a headlock. He wanted to know if I thought he was a word shitter. I told Chicago I had to go—home.

"Leave him alone," Anna said.

Suddenly, Chicago got misty-eyed. He cursed, called this country shit, and said if he could, he'd go back.

"Well then, go back," Uncle Arthúr said. "Plenty of Gypsies there."

Chicago tightened his hold on my head, weighed his words after carefully selecting them: "Screw you," he said to Uncle Arthúr. Then he turned on me. "And you. You think you're an American already, don't you? Don't you?"

"Let him go," Anna said.

"Okey-doke," Chicago said.

My uncle handed me another bottle of Bud.

Chicago pulled my face close to his. He gave me a rough kiss and said, "Go get 'em."

"Where's Jakab?" I asked, scanning the faces in the auditorium. "*He* speaks English doesn't he?"

Chicago smiled and cocked his head toward Uncle Arthúr. "The godfather told the kike to take a hike."

"Why?"

Chicago looked surprised. "You have to ask?"

"Shit," I said.

Chicago said he was leaving. He needed to crash on his cot at the bar and grill. Besides, this was all a lot of bullshit. He asked my uncle for the key. My uncle threw it at him. "Get out of here," he said. "You're drunk."

The Steering Committee sat ominously on the crepe paper stage. The league president was Mr. Alex Bodnár. He was also president of Bodnár & Sons Funeral Parlor. I once saw his picture in the *Cleveland Plain Dealer,* shaking hands with the mayor at an Estonian ball.

Thick tobacco clouds hovered near the ceiling. Despite this being an athletic kind of meeting, the team representatives puffed away like there was no tomorrow, flicking their ashes into beer bottles.

Like the others, I kept my own Bud on the floor, between my ankles. I was uptight as shit. I sipped on the beer and stared at Uncle Arthúr's burning Lucky. "Could I have one of those?"

"Oh, sure." My uncle handed me his pack. I pulled one out. Anna struck a match and cupped it.

Each time league president Bodnár called out Donau-Schwaben, German Americans, Greek Olympians, Hungarian Hunters, Polonia…someone in the audience said, "here" or "*jah.*"

The representative from the Referees' Association went out of his way to give me and my uncle a nasty look. The hall rustled. The league president used his gavel.

An older gentleman who had been straining his arm in the air like a school kid was recognized. "What is it, Friedrich?" the president asked. The old German from Donau-Schwaben got up and announced "This isn't *fussball,* gentlemen."

The league president nodded but looked uneasy. Uncle Arthúr whispered that Friedrich was known to go on and on.

"Sit down," someone from the back yelled. Snickering. The president was again forced to use the gavel.

"That's right," continued Friedrich, turning around. "The Commissioner of Parks and Recreation is not going to keep lending Brookside Field to a bunch of hooligans!"

Uncle Arthúr put his hand on my knee.

I raised my hand, but was ignored. My uncle stood up and said loudly, "No. I am sorry. *Entschuldigen Sie.*"

I let what was left of my cigarette drop into the bottle of Budweiser and stood up with my uncle, ignoring the president's continuous gavel. Persons sitting next to Friedrich pulled him down, so my uncle sat down, leaving me the only one standing.

"The Lake Erie Soccer League recognizes the Hungarian Hunters."

I hesitated. Friedrich and the Romanians and Anna were looking at me.

"Go ahead, use the mike," Uncle Arthúr said. Then his signature lopsided smile: "You're a big boy now. You have a sexy voice."

I unraveled the paper. I was angry. I couldn't go up the middle anymore because of my goddamm English. "The Hungarian Hunters," I heard myself say as I snatched up an eyeful of words, "have willingly and of their own accord suspended Player No. 6 for conduct contrary to the spirit of the sport and to the philosophy of the Hungarian Hunters."

Applause.

I picked up my Bud and took a long pull of what was left—forgetting about the freaking cigarette butt. Instinctively I spat out the bitter juice. I was pissed. Pissed with my uncle for what he was doing to Gypsy. Pissed at the way I was being used. Pissed at the way my uncle and Anna were sucking up to me, just to get rid of Gypsy. I was pissed at Millie. God, I was pissed at her. And I was pissed at myself for being such an asshole. Selling my soul for a cigarette. And the beer! Christ! The bitter freaking beer!

I stood up and spat a wad. "This is what I think of this bullshit," I said.

"Sit down, Art. What the hell—" my uncle hissed.

"My name's not Art," I said. "My name is Attila. Then I turned on him. "You're too cheap to pay for Gypsy's hospital bills so you cut him from the team. What kind of bullshit is that? And you get your freaking Eldorado fixed! What comes first? Huh?"

My uncle tried laughing it off. He must've thought his nephew flipped out. Banged his head. Was talking shit. My uncle's eyes were swimming in blood: "Shut the hell up, you little shit."

I didn't. I ignored the president's gavel and plowed on: "This is bullshit. Bullshit."

"Two beers and he loses it," my uncle said, his arms folded in front of him, his face livid.

"Hear me out, Mr. President," I shouted. I didn't know if it was me talking or my Bud but I didn't give a shit. "My uncle here wants to be an undertaker's understudy. He's getting his Eldorado ready. He's keeping it shiny and new. He wants to suck up to you, sir. You know what his bumper sticker's says, Mr. President? It says, *Undertakers Do It Last!*"

At home, I retreated to my room, locked it and spent most of my time on the bed, staring at the ceiling, thinking about Millie freaking Weiler. What if she really was in Paris? So—this was it. No more Millie. Just like that song on the Elvis album she left me. *Blue freaking Hawaii.* There was a song on it called "*No More,*" and I kept playing it over and over, to the point where it was making me sick.

No more do I feel the touch of your hand in mine

I groaned.

No more do I see the love light making your blue eyes shine

You'd think she'd send me a fucking postcard!

A thousand goodbyes could never put out the embers.

God, what *schmaltz*! *You ain't nothin' but a hound dog* was more like it. In the morning I took the Elvis album and smashed it into pieces. The hell with "*No More.*"

I had to get out of the house and gave Gypsy a call to tell him what happened at the stupid meeting, and to piss and moan about Millie. Gypsy sounded weird. "You didn't see the morning paper," he said.

"What?"

"The *Plain Dealer*, man! Chicago's dead. My brother says it'll be on the six o'clock news. The bar and grill, man, it got blown to smithereens. Chicago's dead, man! Can you believe it?! He's dead!"

"You're shitting me, right? Oh my God!"

"Naw, man. Not about something like this."

"Are they sure it was a bomb?"

"It was something. All it takes is a little nitro and sodium nitrate."

"The Romanians?"

I heard Gypsy's brother bark in the background. "Should've been his goddamm uncle instead of Chicago!"

"Come on, man," Gypsy said to his brother. "It's on the front page. *Local man dies in fire. A pre-dawn blaze at the Hungarian St. Stephen Club Restaurant on the corner of 42nd and Lorain blew out windows, destroyed much of the bar and grill's interior and collapsed the building's roof, killing 28-year-old—*"

"I'm coming over," I said, my adrenaline pumping.

"Wait. Listen to this. *Cleveland Police suspected foul play from the start once the arson squad identified the presence of an accelerant.*"

Neither of us knew what an *accelerant* was, but we did have an idea what Chicago was doing there at the crack of dawn. He had a habit of staying overnight every time he downed one too many, which was often. The poor sonofabitch was trying to play it safe by not driving. Then this.

My folks were in the front yard planting flowers around our new house. I wasn't sure about telling them what happened. I was still pissed at them, plus I had this uneasy feeling in my gut that they'd have some weird ideas about Gypsy being involved. Every time they reminded me that my best friend was a high school dropout and a thug, I'd brag about Gypsy's smarts, his expert knowledge of chemistry and all that. Shit!

On second thought, I decided to let them in on it. I opened the front door and said: "Guess what? A building in the old neighborhood burnt down. They think it's arson."

Without looking up from her planting, my mother said, "Aren't you glad we don't live there anymore. Nothing but crime."

"Guess whose place it is?"

My mother stood up. They were both looking at me now.

"Uncle Arthúr's. Someone blew it up early this morning. Nothing now but a heap of charred rubble. It was on the news. It'll be on again at six. Channel 5."

I watched them look at each other. My mother took off her gardening gloves and gave them to my father. They headed inside, real somber-like.

"They say there was a body. They found a body inside," I said.

"Whose?" my mother asked in horror.

"I don't know. They don't know yet."

'Course all it took was a quick phone call to set their minds at ease about good old Uncle Arthúr. But my father wasn't so sure.

I had to thumb two rides to get to Gypsy's. Lucky for my ass, his brother wasn't at home. We went to the Club to check it out. All the brick was blackened, including the chimney. The entire block was cordoned off. A lone black and white cop car was parked outside. No sign of the patrolman. The place was gutted alright. Like I told my folks, nothing was left but a heap of charred rubble.

We had no idea who could've set the fire. Not a clue, except what the paper said. That it was intentional. The news that evening said little more than the paper. The police were pursuing all leads. A week later Channel 5 News announced that the investigation led to certain persons of interest. It didn't come out for yet another week that the persons of interest were Gypsy and his brother.

The cops went to Gypsy's house twice. They were told they were not suspects, but they should not plan any long trips for a while. Like to Hungary. They also visited Uncle Arthúr. Oh, yeah. I heard from my old man that they asked my uncle about stuff like insurance and shit like that. If my father had any theories on the subject, he kept it to himself.

I knew Gypsy had nothing to do with it. Or his brother. Sure his brother was a psycho, but he wasn't the type. Just a big mouth like Chicago. I felt sorry for Gypsy. He was laying low these days. I thumbed over a few times but we just smoked and listened to his worn-out records. Once or twice we went ice skating to a covered rink that was open year-around. We just weren't into it. Everyone seemed to have a partner on the ice and here we were slipping and sliding solo. After trying some jumps and colliding with a couple, Gypsy said, "Let's get the hell out of here. I could tell he was nervous as shit they'd pin something on him. I wondered how the cops got to Gypsy in the first place. I tried not to think about that too long, because it was probably me. Me and my big ass mouth. Even if they never found the culprit, my folks would think Gypsy had something to do with it. After all, he was a Gypsy!

Jesus Christ! Life was taking a shitty turn. It's been five weeks now! I spent a lot of time walking, brooding, hating my new neighborhood. I got in the habit of sleeping in everyday, jerking off under the covers, in the shower, on the toilet. There had to be some pleasures left in life. I also got in the habit of smoking Camels, the non-filter variety Gypsy smoked. They were a lot stronger than my father's pretentious Parliaments. It didn't take a Surgeon General to know cigarettes weren't any good for me. They certainly weren't doing my spastic heart any good, but, what the hey! My old man was still ticking even though he puffed and hacked away with onc lung.

Life. I was just going through the motions now. I tried not to think of Millie and Paris. I filled up the evenings I didn't work at McDonald's with another part-time job at a place called Ars Medica. My job was to stuff old magazines into an incinerator and watch them burn. I worked only three hours a day but it would take an hour bus ride each way. If this wasn't stupid what was? Sometimes I read into the medical journals I was burning at my new job. I had a field day with diseases, looking for symptoms, eating them up, to the last morbid detail. Despite Dr. Hellerstein's reassurance, I thought I had something wrong with my heart. I read that a definite diagnosis could only be made through procedure called cardiac catherization where they stuck a nylon tube up your groin to your heart. It was not going to happen. I put my heart on the backburner.

Lately I was convinced I had Hodgkins Disease. All I had to do was feel the enlarged node on the side of my neck.

It was a pity, but it couldn't be helped.

In spite of the promise of a new life in a new neighborhood, I would soon die of a terrible cancer that attacked my lymph nodes. My freaking body was turning on me again.

In front of the glowing furnace, I was feverishly leafing through copy after copy of the New England Journal of Medicine. It was Hodgkins, alright. As far as I was concerned no medical tests were needed. Once the tumor in my neck got big enough, it would choke off my air supply, and I'd die by a slow process of strangulation. Hodgkins Disease was a death sentence. I accepted my self-diagnosis on the spot, letting a familiar dark sadness flow into my veins. My face was so hot it felt like it was about to burst into flames like those pages I was tossing into the fire. The edges were curling up one by one in red glowing outlines. I thought about what my uncle said about my aunt freezing to death. Then I felt Chicago's body burn in what must've been the fire from hell when the bar and grill was torched. I remembered the first time he gave me a ride. Every time he shifted he touched my knee. Don't ask me why? But instead of getting out of his car then and there, I let it ride. I don't know whether it was because I didn't want to hurt his feelings or what. Maybe I was a homo and didn't know it. Maybe there was something wrong with me and Millie caught on and got the hell out. My throat ached and my eyes became a watery blur. I took Millie's "To My Hubby" greeting card and tossed it into the flames. Suddenly, I went all sick inside and had to go to the restroom where I had the dry heaves. I flushed.

Another week down the toilet.

Come Sunday, my father cajoled us into going to church with him to the Hungarian Lutheran Church on Denison Avenue. Our car was in the shop for another brake job. Anyway, we were standing by the bus stop in our Sunday best, when a black Pontiac, flaming-detail and all, came barreling down the street and headed straight at us. It happened so fast we had no time to react. It missed the curb and us by inches, but the sonofabitch managed to splash all three of us in the process. We ended up having to walk back home, take off our dripping suits and wipe out our ears. My old man was convinced it was not a prank. When I called his bluff and told him to call the cops, he said it wouldn't do any good, since none of us had a read on the plates. Man, did he latch on to that careening Pontiac, blaming it on all the unusual suspects, and he yacked about it obsessively all week.

On the weekend we had visitors. An old friend of my father from his college days, with his wife and daughter. They were passing through town on their way to Florida and spent a few days with us. At supper, after several rounds of *pálinka*, my father and his friend reminisced about the good old days at Franz Joseph University. I was surprised to find out my father was regarded as a "bohemian" who was quite the ladies' man. At one time, he was hounded by creditors who showed up at his college apartment to take his expensive Persian rug. "Mercifully," my father's friend said, "the creditors took pity on your father since he was using it to protect himself from the cold. In those days, your father slept on the floor. His creditors had already repossessed his bed."

Wow. I wondered if that was the same rug with the swastika in the center but I thought I'd better not ask, because before long, my father steered the conversation toward the world Zionist conspiracy.

The daughter who was positioned to sit next to me was hideous. She was fat and lumpy and sank into the chair like a sack of potatoes. She had no waist, no neck, and no chin. What she did have was this enormous beak which curved at the end into a meaty bulb. Her eyes were way too far apart, and she had thick black hair, the kind you couldn't comb, no matter what you did with it, the kind that looked like it was torn out of a mattress. This girl was sitting there, dumbly twiddling her thumbs in her lap. Now and then when she thought her father said something funny, she'd flash an idiot smile exposing sharp little teeth. She was 14, going on 15. My father got up from the table and winked at me as he brushed by my chair, saying, "She's really something, isn't she?"

Yeah, a real dodo bird. For the next few days, I was forced to endure a painful family outing to the Art Museum and a photo shoot with me and the dodo bird. Compared to her, Millie was a swan. We had our picture taken by the Art Museum all the time, but we never bothered to go inside. The fun continued. We took a marathon trip to Niagara Falls, with the windows up the whole way. We took two cars. That's what my family did with visitors, take them to the Art Museum and to Niagara Falls, a three-day affair under the best of circumstances, just to see water falling down. We had to do both sides, the American and the Canadian side, where we had supper. It was in the wee hours of the morning when the caravan arrived in Cleveland.

The next day, I found a letter in our mailbox addressed to me.

My heart was pounding as I tore open the envelope. It was not from Millie. All the note said was, "Call me." It was signed Kitty Miller.

Kitty Miller? I had to rake my memory. I had trouble placing her. Kitty? The girl on our double date? The Friendship Formal. Eons ago. Shit. Maybe word got out that Millie and me were no longer an item. That she was in Paris. It was a depressing thought. Anyway, I took my chances and dialed the number. Kitty answered. She said Millie called her and she wanted to see me. Would I meet her in front of the Museum of Art Saturday at noon, by the museum steps?

I knew it. In the pit of my stomach I knew Paris was all bullshit. Other than the message, Kitty knew nothing else about Millie, no phone, no nothing.

Friday, I called my coach to tell him I wouldn't be able to make Saturday's game because I had mono. Fever. Swollen glands. Lassitude.

Coach told me I was cut from the team and it wasn't so much because I missed a shitload of practice and several key games, but because I was freelancing for the Hungarian Hunters. He knew one of the refs and heard about my unsportsmanlike conduct. He said it didn't surprise him. I could be brutal. But during practice? There was no call for it. I was to hand in my uniform and clean out my locker ASAP.

Screw him. And screw soccer. There were more important things in life. Saturday turned out to be one of those once-in-a-blue-moon days without a cloud in the sky. The steel mills took a break from spewing their volcanic ash into the air, and you could see for miles. As the train pulled out of the Terminal Tower tunnel, the sunlight appeared overly bright. I was melting in my turtleneck and afraid for the box of Fanny Farmer chocolates I had with me.

The ride was endless. I was used to riding from one end of the line to the other without much bother. It was different now. The last time I made the trip in my futile search for Millie, it didn't seem half as long. The connecting shuttle, plastered with sunflowers since I last saw it, was right on schedule. I realized the shuttle route had a stop not far from the college soccer field where we played our first game against Ohio State a month and a half ago. That's how long Millie kept me in the dark. To think she'd been here all this time!

I smoked a couple of cigarettes on the steps of the museum as I scanned the sidewalk along East Boulevard and the winding path around the lagoon.

She was running late. Five minutes, then ten. When I spotted her I rushed down the steps. The first thing I noticed was her black sunglasses. They were enormous. She wore a blue raincoat and this crazy red bandana.

We hugged, but there was no kiss. Millie appeared very nervous.

"Why didn't you call me?" I said angrily.

She couldn't, she said. It was her father. She said he hired a detective who was watching her 24 hours a day. We were being watched right now. We had to be careful.

I looked around. Just for the hell of it. "What about all that marriage stuff?"

"Calm down."

"I am calm. I just want to know where the fuck I stand. You could've called."

She said she did call, but I was never home or the number wouldn't work.

"That's a lot of shit, and you know it!"

She asked me why I was talking like that, using language like that. She said she just wants to hold on to my arm and walk. We walked around the lagoon. The museum grounds were a blur. Millie said she couldn't call before, because she was afraid for me, that I would be arrested. "My Dad told me he'd have you arrested for statutory rape."

"Bullcrap. I was at the Fairview Police station. Yeah. Your old man reported me. The cop just asked me a few questions like, were you easy? Real nice guy, this father of yours."

"He didn't. My God!" Millie burst out crying.

I did not put my arm around her. "You still could've called. I mean what does it take to make a goddamm call? The cop said you gave him instructions for me not to contact you." My hand trembled as I fired up another cigarette.

"I swear to God I did no such thing." Millie's eyes were clouded over with tears. Her mascara was running. "Please, don't be angry with me, Art. My father said he had your telephone tapped at your house. And my dorm phone is tapped and—"

"My name is Attila now."

"Alright. Attila."

"Christ Almighty, Millie! Who d'you think your old man is? Almighty God? Shit! You freaking abandon me and the best you can do is this stupid shit paranoia. Jesus. One of my professors is a Hungarian nut case who thinks the CIA is bugging his phone, too. My own father's paranoid. I'm up to my ass with this shit. It's just too much. Too much, man! I didn't know where on God's earth you were. Or if you were okay. One day you're a big married woman sending me "Hubby" greeting cards, the next you're Daddy's frightened little baby. Which one is it?"

She was sobbing by now. Then, between breaths: "I'm so nervous, I think I'm having a nervous breakdown."

"No, you're not."

"I am too. I'm taking tranquilizers. I can't concentrate on anything at school. I don't sleep. I'm tired all the time. My hands shake so much I can't hold a pencil. You have no idea what I've been going through."

"You have no idea what I've been going through. I had to call in sick and miss a soccer game just to get here. There goes my freaking scholarship!"

"Please don't yell at me. Can we just talk about this normally?"

One thing I didn't feel like was talking normally. I wanted to torture her, to make her feel the same shit she put me through. I wondered if she was capable of feeling anything, any freaking thing. I hated it when she was numb. God, how I hated it. My ranting forced the swans to make a beeline toward the center of the lagoon.

We sat down on a bench.

"You haven't even asked what happened to me," Millie cried. "Do you even care? After we got caught my father went crazy. I was locked in my room. I was terrified of what he'd do next. He was a raging lunatic. He tore up our album. It was all there in the morning for me to see. Torn to pieces, scattered on the floor. All our pictures. Everything. My graduation picture. Everything. Then my Dad went out looking for you with a baseball bat. God! You don't know him. He gets physical! He used to beat me. And they weren't just love taps. I'd scream for my mother for help but she didn't do anything. She'd just watch. They're like a team. When they finally decided to speak to me, the first thing my parents asked was if that was the first time you fucked me. That's the word they used. 'Fuck.' They made it seem so vulgar. I tried to explain to them that I loved you. I didn't tell them we were married."

"Why not?"

"I knew they wouldn't...understand." Millie started herself on a fresh deluge of tears. "My parents thought it was very funny when I told them I loved you. They wanted to take me to the doctor to make sure I wasn't pregnant. I told them it wasn't necessary.

"They said I couldn't be trusted going to away to school. And I was supposed to start Monday the same as you. Fine with me, I thought. But I was determined to get out somehow and be with you. Get a job if I had to, get an apartment. Leave.

"They said Art School was out. That I ruined it. That I was a whore. That I broke their hearts. I was never to see you again, and if you ever came around, my Dad was going to kill you."

"Let him try."

Millie caught her breath. "The next day they told me they changed their minds. I could go to Art School, after all. But not before my mother gave me a little talk. You know what she said? I was so hurt, I couldn't believe it. My mother said there were lots of girls out there who were not virgins. What did she think I was? Some kind of whore? She wanted me to start dating fraternity guys. Then they brought me here and dumped me. Nobody's been here since. No visits. Nothing. And I have trouble making friends." Her voice faltered. "I overheard my roommate tell one of her friends that I was spaced out all the time. She used the word 'zombie'."

"Your mother said you were in goddamm Paris. What was I supposed to think when I was in the hospital with a goddamm concussion."

"Hospital?"

"I got banged up in a soccer game. What do you care?"

"I do care."

"If you cared you would've called. You could've told a friend or called a friend to call me. Or you could've dropped a line. Or does your Dad have the U.S. Post Office in his pocket too? You can't tell me there was absolutely no way to, to—"

Millie took out a worn hanky and dabbed at her eyes. "I guess I was panicky," she said. She looked at me. "Will you forgive me?"

I sighed and said "yes." I'd rather believe anything, including her breakdown than the possibility that she didn't care enough to call or write. (What about public freaking phones and post freaking cards? Christ.) I didn't want to think about it.

But I did.

Millie was not only nervous but cool. She was afraid of intimacy. When I tried kissing her, she got paranoid.

Shit! Now I was angry.

I stood up abruptly and tossed my half-smoked cigarette into the lagoon. "Shit, you wanted to get caught."

"What?"

"You could've locked the damned door like I told you. You kept saying Bonnie would bark. Well, your dog Bonnie freaking let us down."

"You're crazy."

"Why would you do it in your house when your father calls you a whore for kissing me? Why give his rubbers to me to use? Why?"

"Stop it!" Millie screamed.

But I kept going, rubbing it in until she snapped. And when she snapped she got physical and landed a barrage of blows on my ears.

That was the extent of our physical contact that day.

I took the train back with my ears ringing. I swore her off. Freaking violent, man! Who was the barbarian now, goddammit Christ?! She could go to hell. As far as I was concerned, the entire sick Rottweiler pack could go to hell.

CHAPTER 9

A week went by. I didn't call. She didn't call. On Thursday I received a letter from her written in green ink.

Dear Attila,

I wanted to call you but something is still wrong with your telephone. An operator keeps saying it's an unpublished number. I wanted to tell you that I'm sorry. I'm sorry for my stupid silliness. I was scared, maybe more scared than I should've been. Please don't remind me over and over again how it was my fault we got caught. I know it was. Attila, if you want me to stay sane, please don't remind me of it. I couldn't bear that now. I need you now. Please have patience with me. I am going to show you that I love you. Please know that you're the most important person in my life. And always will be. I love you.

She signed it "*Bocsáss meg*," Hungarian for "Forgive me."

A warm feeling came over me. Nobody I cared for ever told me they were sorry. Not my mother. Not my aunt. Nobody. I didn't think the word existed in Hungarian. Now I knew better. So—Millie did try to call me. It was my stupid old man. He was changing our phone numbers left and right. Half the time I didn't know my own number. I wanted Millie to know how much her letter meant to me. How much she meant to me. I called her. She cried so hard, she barely got the words out. She didn't want to tell me when I visited. She was becoming unglued. She was so upset, she didn't want to tell me in a letter, but she couldn't wait any longer. She was going crazy. She thought she was pregnant.

I could hear my heart beating in my ears. "Again?" I said.

"I've never been this late. It's a month and a half," she said between sobs.

I tried calming her by saying it was just stress. I was feeling it myself but didn't let on. Sweat started running down my back. This time it was different, she said. She'd been to the doctor and although it was too early to tell, she knew she was pregnant.

I felt like saying, "No you're not," but I didn't. Not this time. Something told me I better get my ass over there. I told her I'd take the first train running so we could figure out what to do. She said "okay" in a shaky voice.

I met her at the Western Reserve University cafeteria at the crack of dawn. They just finished setting up the chairs. I asked her if she wanted to eat anything, and she said no, just coffee. Black. Her stomach wasn't doing real well lately. She was pretty shaken up. She had this feeling, call it "sixth sense." "What are we going to do?" she asked, her eyes liquid, her face red.

"There's only one thing to do," I said. "I'll quit school and get a job."

"I can't ask you to do that," she said.

The way things stood, it wasn't like I was going to school or anything, I told her. I reassured her about taking care of her and the baby. I said it like I meant it. Maybe I could take some courses at night and try and finish school. If it came down to making a choice between my illustrious medical career and Millie and the baby, it was no contest.

We never brought up abortion, not because it was illegal or that we were Jesus freaks or anything like that. We just didn't. I knew my plans were half-baked and all that, but I was all set to prove my love, and in a big way. I was glad Millie had no idea how much of a wreck I was inside about the whole thing and glad she didn't ask for specifics. Like how I planned to take care of her and the baby. She just pressed my hand and said, "I know you will." She let out a huge sigh and looked at the menu. Her appetite came back, as did mine. We had English muffins, scrambled eggs and sausage patties. I felt good, like I was needed. I told her I never had English muffins before. They tasted pretty decent with strawberry jam.

We saw each other every day that week. I would cut the shit out of my biology and calculus classes. I was flunking them anyhow. She'd meet me on the museum steps and we'd continue walking and talking. Millie was getting better about letting me touch her and kiss her, but when I tried to go further by kissing her with my tongue, her teeth came between us. She was still paranoid about us being watched and she was spooked about being pregnant. So was I. The difference was that I happened to be a freaking fatalist. If she really was pregnant, what was the big deal about doing it? I wouldn't have to worry about using a condom or pulling it out.

She said she was done playing Russian roulette. I got pissed and said something like, "Fine by me." Then she tried to backtrack, asking me to be patient, asking for more time.

We cooled it, took a long walk up and around Murray Hill. I was telling her about the insane soccer brawl and the restaurant fire. Up till now I was tight-lipped about Gypsy being a suspect. The poor sucker was upgraded from being a person of interest to a bona fide suspect. "The cops must've found something," I said to Millie. "Now they're pretty sure it was a bomb. The crazy thing is Gypsy is weirdly excited about it. That the cops would think he had the goods and the smarts to be a munitions expert. Not bad for a high school dropout."

Millie asked about our friend who got killed in the fire.

"Yeah," I said. "I told Gypsy there was something wrong with the picture, like Chicago, and he got pissed. I can't figure Gypsy out. I mean here's a guy who thinks he's a great chemist and all, and he has no idea what an accelerant is."

"He sure knows what an accelerator is," Millie tried to lighten things up. "What is…what's that other word?"

"Accelerant. Something that speeds up a fire. I looked it up."

Millie asked about Chicago.

"He was at the wrong place at the wrong time. He was a nice guy, kind of a hot dog and a loudmouth, but okay. I was there when he got the key from my uncle. The key to the bar and grill. The way things turned out, my uncle gave the poor guy the key to hell. They ended up sending his ashes back to Hungary. To be sprinkled over his mother's grave. How freaky is that? From what Chicago told me, his mother died not long after he split for the U.S. of A. He was in his twenties when he started a new life in Chicago."

"Sad. I guess a lot of families got separated around that time," Millie said. "You know, you never told me how you and your mother were reunited. After you escaped."

I told Millie about the Red Cross, how we put my mother's and my brother's name on a list of missing persons, just in case they crossed the border. "We even got to make a short announcement on the air on a Red Cross radio station. It was cool. One refugee after another, saying he or she was safe and was looking for so and so. It took some time, but we found them. They were in Salzburg in a *lager*. That's what Austrians call a camp. That's where we were eventually reunited.

"We were pretty happy to be together. The food in the *lager* was enough to feed the state of Ohio, if only it tasted decent. No English muffins there. We were fed these bland noodles out of a can. Slab after slab of over-salted yellow butter. Fluorescent green Jello. We were used to hardy meals, you know, like head cheese, but this, this green thing they called Jello, really took the cake. My mother said it tasted like the smell of insect repellant. She said she wasn't about to eat anything that trembled before you touched it. Now my mother's pork aspic—which is a lot like Jello, except with a wonderful meat base—now that was a hardy meal in winter. We were glad as shit to have her back."

"Meat Jello? Yuck. Sounds awful."

"You should try it sometime. Anyway, we spent our evenings in the same room sitting or lying on our bunk beds, chewing on pieces of soggy bread or sipping bitter lukewarm tea from aluminum cups. Sometimes me and János were lucky enough to get jelly on our bread. Strawberry jam would've been great but jelly was better than nothing. It was just that the jelly tasted a lot like their Jello. The color was a brilliant red never seen in nature. It tasted like it, too.

"My mother sewed little Hungarian flags out of felt and she sent my brother and me into town to see if we could exchange them for *schillings*. 'Ask some nice Austrian policeman,' she'd say. 'Be polite. Always say *Danke Schön*'."

"I guess I had the balls to go up to the gendarmes and pester them for money so my mother could buy things like lard and paprika to doctor up our bland meals. János begged off. He thought it was beneath him to go begging in the new country. He'd rather spend his time climbing the hills nearby, or playing tag in the *lager*'s empty swimming pool. The Red Cross outfitted every kid under the age of 16 with a wool overcoat, sweaters from Ireland, leather shoes from England, berets from France. The week before Christmas, toys arrived by the truckloads, mountains of shit piled high in a ware-house. The kids were just let loose. It was great.

"When I got my first baseball glove, a gift from the children of America, I didn't know what to make of it. Where was the other glove? Did they think I was left-handed?"

After walking our asses off around Murray Hill, me and Millie came full circle and realized we were back by the lagoon and our favorite bench. Sitting down felt good. Millie said it was a real trip when I talked about all the crazy shit that happened to me. Her life was just normal and boring, she said.

"Come on."

"Well, I didn't have anything like that happen to me. I told you about my uncle with the Purple Heart. That's about it. He was my father's half-brother. My father couldn't join the Army because of his arm. He broke it as a kid, and it was never set right. I think my Dad felt bad he had to stay at home, when all his friends were out there fighting for their country. I'm a baby boomer like you. My mother sent me to a Catholic school, and because I was tall for my age, the stupid nuns always put me in the back of the class. I hated it. They scared the living daylights out of me. I don't think I talked once in grade school. I told you I had the same problem you had with the nuns. They were quick to condemn my Dad for not being a Catholic. There was a lot of pressure. My mom was drinking by then, but she's a pretty good cook. She makes a pretty good roast Sundays—and Jello salad—in case you're interested. Hot rolls and, oh, I almost forgot, shrimp cocktail. We usually have that before dinner. I love shrimp cocktail. Did you ever have shrimp cocktail? My Dad and mom usually have martinis before dinner but since my Dad found out he's diabetic it's just my mom. She drinks enough for both of them, I guess," Millie laughed. "That's about it. Oh, I didn't like school till I got to public school and got involved with art. My parents always thought I was good enough to go to Paris to study. Geez, I have enough problems keeping up with the work over here. These Art School kids are way ahead of me. I don't know. My Dad wasn't always like this. Sometimes I think it's his diabetes and blood pressure that's making him angry all the time."

I told Millie that was probably what it was. "You really think he hired a private detective to tail us? I mean, it's pretty crazy."

"You don't know my Dad. Anyway, I don't want to talk about him. I want to talk about you." Millie wanted to know what it was like when I first got here.

"Oh, you mean Cleveland? We thought it was the ugliest city in the world. All those chimneys, steel mills, the salt flats. Tinker-toy bridges. Compared to the Chain Bridge over the Danube and the neo-gothic Parliament, Cleveland scared the shit out of us. We first lived in the inner city, with its graffiti and rusty fire escapes. Funny, I still miss it. Most of my classmates were Puerto Ricans. One of them pulled a knife on me once for fouling him in a pick-up basketball game. Oh yeah, the first day of school, my very first day of school in Cleveland, I got lost on my way home. Shit, was I stupid. My mother told me to wait for my brother, but no, I had to show everybody I knew my way. I ended up by a cemetery on the other side of town. This is after walking my little butt off in the rain. I retraced my steps and finally found a main thoroughfare I recognized. Lorain Avenue. The longest avenue in Cleveland, if not the world. Christ, everything's on Lorain Avenue. So I went into the first bar on Lorain Avenue where I heard Hungarian spoken and asked for help. A nice man volunteered to take me home. He treated me to my first Coke and a bag of potato chips. They tasted pretty strange, salty as all get-out. Then he ordered me a hot-dog with the works. By the time he got me home I was stuffed. By my second week, I was already swiveling on one of those red stools in Woolworth's and getting a tall glass of iced tea. I took back some empty bottles, enough, I guess, to get me a tall glass of iced tea.

"My parents' first job was at this private Hungarian club. My father tended bar, my mother cooked. In a year we saved enough to put a down payment on a house on Whitman Avenue, still the inner city but it was ours. We bought our first TV and our first car ever, a four-door Chrysler. My mother got her hairdresser's license and eventually got her own shop. When I was 12, she made me go into her shop all summer because she didn't trust me at home. God, I was bored out of my freaking mind. She said she needed me to translate in case someone wanted something different than a shampoo and set. They never did. I spent the whole summer leafing through old *TV Guides* and going crazy. There was an old piano in the basement. As a last resort I'd go down and play this yellow piano with missing keys, pretending I was a famous composer. I had to sweep up hair, rid hair from rollers and shit like that. Man, instead playing baseball or soccer, I was trapped in a beauty shop with a bunch of old ladies who smelled like freaking hair spray. Makes me tired just talking about it. The rest, you know. My brother and I were sent crosstown to Cathedral Latin. We're both supposed to be doctors. I think I'm supposed to be a heart specialist and my brother a brain surgeon. Whew! I think I'd rather be a papa. What do you think?"

"You'd make a great papa."

"Cool," I said.

The papa thing was cool and all that. It's just that when I got up from the bench, everything turned black in front of me. I had to wait a moment to regain my balance. We must've been sitting for a long time, or maybe it was because we hadn't eaten anything.

We went to a little supermarket on Euclid so Millie could get a couple of things for the kitchenette in the dorm. When we came to a shelf where they kept the sugar, I told Millie how my mother would take a pin with her when she first went shopping so she could poke holes in the packages to find out which was the sugar and which was the salt. "There was this one thing we were really nuts about," I told Millie. "Toasters. We'd never seen anything like it. We were amazed how the toaster popped up the bread. We would spend an entire day making nothing but toast. It wasn't all fun and games, though."

I told Millie about the first time we hosted our American neighbors for dinner. "Talk about a fiasco! My mother was in the middle of making chicken paprikash when she sent me to the corner drug store for some napkins. Something nice. Something special. I went to Marshall Drug on the corner and came back with some pretty fancy stuff, alright. A nice blue box with a rose on the corner. 'Course I didn't know that what I bought home were feminine napkins. So, while my parents and bother struggled with their scrappy English to entertain our American guests, I was setting the table, placing our best silverware on top of the frigging Kotex. My mother had a cow. What would our neighbors think? *Jézus Mária!*"

Millie laughed her ass off. She wanted to know what women used in the old country. "Rags," I said. "And for the outhouse in the village, we used newspapers. My father loved wiping his ass with all that propaganda shit. In the winter we used snowballs. The summer I was there, it was so hot, the smell in the shithouse had so many green flies it drove me up a tree."

"Gross," Millie said.

"No. I'm serious, man. It drove me up a tree. I climbed a tree and did it from a branch. It was nice and breezy up there among the leaves. And when the shit fell on the sand, it curled like shit in kitty litter. The leaves made for great toilet paper. It was very sanitary. There was nothing uncivilized about it."

I think she said "zany" or something like that. Then lowering her voice she said, "Oh, before I forget, I want to ask you, would you buy some tampons for me? I'm always so embarrassed. It's crazy."

I lit up like a Christmas tree. "You got your period??"

"Shhh. No. No! But just in case. If I do get it, it'll be heavy. I have some in my purse but I thought I better get some more. Would you buy it for me? Here's the money. I can't help it. I get embarrassed. Usually I have my Dad get them for me. While you're at it, could you get me a roll of Charmin toilet paper?"

The letdown struck me like a sledge hammer. And now I had to play fetch! Jesus freaking Christ! I thought. That's what I get for playing Russian roulette. You better get used to it, boy, I told myself. It won't be long before you're changing diapers.

So—I was back in the shithouse, pretending to be a young dad with a pipe. *Father Knows Best.*

I got her the tampons and the Charmin. She waited for me outside the store. I asked Millie if she ever had to use an outhouse. It wasn't out of spite or anything. Just a question. Just a freaking question.

"Maybe my great grandfather," she laughed. "And he lived in Germany."

"I suppose you always had blue water in your toilet so you won't have to face the good old yellow color of what most people know as piss."

"As a matter of fact, yes," she said. And her grandparents who lived in Shaker Heights even had a *bidet*. That was French. When she described how it worked it sounded like it was something I'd like to try.

I told her it sounded like she had a pretty pampered childhood, to which she answered, "Ah, I don't think so." She had some horror stories of her own. When she was just a baby and her Dad was feeding her spaghetti, she tossed most of it on the floor and made a mess. Her Dad's response was to flip the bowl over. On her head. She had to wear the bowl like a beanie with these yucky wet noodles hanging like dreadlocks—until her Dad took a picture. A real Kodak moment.

"It's child abuse," I said. Then I realized Millie wasn't laughing. "I'm sorry. What is with that Dad of yours? You know, when I first met you, I didn't think you had any respect for your parents, that you were just being a brat, like most American kids. So, I guess things are not always groovy on Cromwell Avenue."

"Not even close. You don't know the half of it." There was something else. More painful than humiliating. I was surprised she could remember back that far. "My mom and Dad were getting ready to go out, and my Dad was changing my diaper and did something pretty scary."

Here Millie's eyes welled up. "I guess my Dad lost his patience. I was still wearing diapers at three. My Dad deliberately stuck me in the hip with the safety pin.

"Jesus," I said. "Are you sure? Where was your mother all this time?"

"Where she always was. With a bottle. And it wasn't the baby bottle."

Her mother was weird, Millie said. She wanted Millie to start dating when she was 12. At 14, her mother wanted her to have a boob job. "Can you beat that?! My God!! It's a good thing my grandmother told her where to get off. Without my grandmother, I'd be a basket-case."

In my case, it was too late, I told Millie. "I'm already a basket-case. Whatever sanity I have left is because of my aunt. The trouble is my memory of her is pretty hazy. Come to think of it, my whole childhood is a blur. Don't ask me why. When I got whacked on the head during the soccer brawl I told you about, I had these weird-ass dreams?"

"Like what?"

"You don't want to hear this shit."

"I do so."

"They're more like flashbacks. All part of the concussion, I guess. I'm always this little kid. And I'm always naked. Weird. It's at my aunt's apartment in Budapest. I'm like this Dennis the Menace except I'm butt naked. I think I told you my mother wanted a girl. Well, she did. She cried every time she saw me naked. I guess that's why she shipped me off to my aunt who not only didn't mind, she actually liked it."

"You're kidding, right."

"Right."

"So you were a little Attila the Hunk."

"Not you, too! Give me a break!"

"I will, if you tell me about your girlfriends. A hunk like you. Attila the Hunk. Attila the Hunk. Don't tell me you didn't have any girlfriends before I came along."

"Forget about me for a change, what about you? You started dating, when? At 12? You know what I was doing at 12. Oh, yeah, I told you. Hey, what time is it anyway? My shift at McDonald's starts…now?! Aw shit! Can you call and tell them I'm in Pittsburgh or something?"

Millie called, and they told her that if I wasn't there in 30 minutes I was fired. No way was I going to make it, so we decided to screw the job and get a pizza. We headed over to Little Italy for some New York style pizza and Coke. Millie paid for it by check, drawn on her father's account. She said her father owed her. She'd been working at his Putt-A-Round course for three years and never got paid.

I felt crummy about sponging off Millie. The thing is I had some money now and then, but it was mostly then. My checks from my part-time jobs went straight into my mother's account, earmarked for my education.

Which was looking pretty bleak these days. My average was 1.38. Automatically I was placed on academic probation. At least, I was smart enough not to show my report card to my old man, dumping it instead straight into our garage incinerator. But my guilt made me keep lugging the freaking medical book everywhere I went. If nothing else, I was strengthening my biceps.

I was faring better in my love life. At least, there I was getting off probation. Millie wanted me to stay longer and longer. The next day, McDonald's had a rush and I was rehired. But by that time, I wasn't interested. Millie told me she'd spoken to the House Mother at her dorm, and I could now call for her. I was only allowed as far as the lobby where I was to announce myself. Nothing personal, just the rules of the Agnus Gund House.

The Agnes Gund House was an old, ivy-covered building set among the fancy-ass estates of Fraternity Row. On the day of my visit, the Sig Eps across the street had the volume up and the fraternity house throbbed with the Beatles' "Money."

> *You know the best things in life are free*
> *But you could leave 'em to the birds and the bees*

I wondered if Millie found any of the guys in the fraternity interesting. She told me she went there once with her roommate. They were all jerks, she said. Beer-guzzling jerks. When they didn't drink beer, they talked about drinking beer. As for her fellow art students, they were a pretty radical bunch, according to Millie. Some were militant peaceniks with peace-sign armbands who not only protested the Vietnam War but wanted to beat up on anyone who wore a tie. Their favorite word was "Fascist." And there were the starving artists who believed you had to look like an artist to be one, rich punks just hanging out, forking out extra cash for the worn look of faded jeans. Millie didn't fit in with any of them.

I crossed the street as two Sig Eps were tossing the football on the front lawn. They both wore sweatshirts with Greek letters and tight bell-bottoms. They were both barefoot. The taller one sported long beautiful hair parted in the middle and a soft-looking beard. It was like watching Jesus Christ play touch football. The other guy had a pretty face that came with a tiny nose and wholesome pink chipmunk cheeks, the kind you'd like to pinch. By contrast, I felt I had a bird beak for a nose. I was a hawk, a predator. My rough-cut cheekbones were hacked out of granite. I was sullen and solitary. My theme song was not "Money" but "King of the Road." Yup, I looked more like a homeless bum, more like a barbarian of the steppes than a college man. Let's face it, as a college student, I was a joke. But as a vagabond, I could have a certain charm. I was doing a lot of gallivanting around these days, and if there was a detective on my tail, he was going to have a problem with blisters.

> *Trailers for sale or rent*
> *Rooms to rent fifty cents*
> *Two hours of pushing broom gives me*
> *Eight by ten one-bedroom*
> *I'm a man of means by no means, king of the road.*

I was king of the Rapid-Transit. King of the *steppes* leading up to the Cleveland Museum of Art. Oarsman among the lagoon's water lilies and quacking ducks. Quack. Quack.

Here I was in front of the Agnes Gund House's massive door. I collected myself in my threadbare sweater and the tie with the fleurs-de-lis.

I pressed the buzzer. Something clicked, and the door opened on its own. I announced myself to the empty lobby: Attila the Great, King of the Steppes, here to see the Millie Weiler, Artist-in-Residence.

There was a phone on the wall. I picked it up and asked for Millie. The voice on other end asked, "The CIA student?"

"W-What?"

"The Cleveland Institute of Art student."

"Oh. Yeah."

Millie flitted down the stairs in a short-sleeved top and light pants with these freaky little spring flowers. Her dark hair smelled fresh. She was holding a sketch pad. Her eyes lit up when she saw me.

We walked arm in arm to our usual place by the museum and the lagoon where the trees were blooming now. They smelled sweet and peppery at the same time. Today it was warm enough to lie on the grass, and I put my sweater down for Millie. I loved the ribbon in her hair, I loved her light cotton pants without the girdle, the soft pressure of her legs.

Millie was showing me her latest sketches, page after page of what looked to me like a series of colored wheels. She said some were passion flowers, some haloes of the Virgin Mary. She did them in various styles, abstract, Impressionist, stylized, etc. For her design class.

"Well??" she asked.

"It's different."

"Thanks for the compliment." Millie picked up her sketch book and leafed through it breezily. "Do you think I'm any good?"

I took the sketch book from her hand and studied her passion flowers. She had a very fine hand. I mean, her lines were really sharp. I liked them. I lit a cigarette and kept it in my mouth. I held the brilliantly colored wheels at arms' length. It looked like she took her time. The colors in the tiny wheels were brilliant, like shards of stained glass. She was light years ahead of my uncle's haphazard strokes. I told her I liked them. A lot.

"You'd better."

We munched on popcorn, fed the ducks. We kissed each other with salty lips. We went inside the museum to see their Egyptian exhibit.

Toward dusk, we looked for a secluded spot. One of the walks around the museum grounds led to a hidden path that wound down an embankment of grass and stone. A cavity cut into the mossy blocks looked perfect. A large oak tree with its roots spreading down the embankment made it even more secluded. Standing, we fit the hollow snugly. Which meant we had to do it standing up, but that didn't seem to bother us.

Millie was just stepping out of her flowered pants when we heard something. Up in the tree, among the leaves.

"Oh God," Millie said.

Someone was watching us from the tree. It wasn't a detective but a homeless man. Jerking off, watching us.

"Pervert!" I shouted.

The man slithered off the tree and lumbered out of sight, but the spell was broken. Millie was afraid again.

"Freaking pervert!" I said.

Without her realizing it, Millie peed in her panties and she wasn't laughing. She was crying. We headed to the Reserve Library, where they had a john.

Millie took her sweet old time in the lavatory. I did a quick browse through a section on mythology. Nothing per se on Hungarian myth, and much less on any magic horn. Then I looked up Attila the

Hun in the *Catholic Encyclopedia*, only to find a small paragraph, most of it devoted to how Pope Leo saved Western civilization by showing the barbarian the one true Cross at the River Mincius.

When I asked the woman at the information desk about the Huns, she led me to an oversized reference book of World War II propaganda posters. I found my "Huns." Portrayed as monsters wielding bloody swords over infants. STOP THE HUNS! STOP THE NAZI HUNS! BUY U.S. SAVINGS BONDS!

Millie came up behind me, I slammed the book shut. My face was red. I told her she took a long time. I wanted to go back to where we left off, but she nixed it. "I'm sorry. I am. But I just can't."

In silence we headed back to the Agnes Gund House. Attila the Great was not going to get any tonight. It was just as well. I was warm all over and angry and confused.

Before we said goodbye at the train station, I had what Millie called my usual conniption fit. I accused her of not loving me enough. "What's with you?" I snapped. "Why are you such a prick teaser? You get a kick out of it. I think you get a kick out of it."

"You're going to start up again, aren't you?"

"What? So now I can't express my feelings. Just because you don't have any, is that it? That's it, isn't it? You can't feel, even if you tried. You can't love. You won't make love because you can't love. You're not into it, you just go through the motions. But you won't even do that anymore. Why bother? You're the coldest bitch I've ever known, I swear to God." I picked on her like this until she cried. Once she cried, I stopped. But first I had to see real tears. Then, and only then, did I tell her I was sorry, that I was frustrated. Hurt.

It was a pattern with me. Every time we had to separate, I threw a tantrum, only to regret it later on the long brooding train ride home. God, how I hated going home on the train. What was it with trains and me? How could I be such a heartless prick? All of a sudden, the freaking reincarnation of Attila the Great wasn't funny anymore.

Millie didn't do anything wrong. Why did I have to make her cry like that?

Why did I feel like she was abandoning me all over again? Just because she didn't want to have sex with me? I was the one leaving. I'd be back tomorrow. Something about leaving on a train, and watching the wheels. A vague pain was sharpening inside me into a cutting edge and I had no idea where it was coming from.

I tried distracting myself by zeroing in on the face of an old woman on the otherwise empty train. She was talking to her reflection in the window. I felt sorry for her. For some reason, she reminded me of my mother, and all the trains and all the freaking goodbyes. If only I didn't feel so much. Outside, there was nothing but darkness and the rain pelting the window. My features in the steamy glass highlighted the pores on my face. The magnified image scared the shit out of me. I was looking at the skin of a reptile. An absurd close-up of my Uncle Arthúr's porous skin. I could count the hairs on his nose. In the dark glass my own skin was porous and hairy like my uncle's. There was another image. A naked little kid with long yellow hair was making a dash for the window in the Párisi street bedroom. The glass shattered and his ceramic heart broke into a thousand cutting edges. *Az agybaj nagybaj*, I heard my father say. *A mental case is a basket-case.* And I was going to take care of Millie and the baby.

I reached into my bag for paper and pen and started scribbling away, the only way I knew to make the cutting edges go away. I was still working on the same poem when the conductor told me it was the end of the line.

It was literally the end of the line for me, in more ways than one. Because of my freaking grades, I received a letter from Uncle Sam, something which I didn't tell Millie. I was too scared. I was about to become 1-A, and I could be drafted at the drop of Uncle Sam's hat. So said a very official notice from my branch of the Selective Service.

At least now I had something concrete to be afraid of. Not so much playing war in the jungle with real bullets, but having to leave Millie and the baby. Christ, it was a screwed up world! Freaking stupid. Of course I was stupid, too. If only I'd listen to my folks and hit the books. If only my parents had listened to me about coming to a warlike country like America. If only my brother had listened when we played cowboys and Indians. Didn't I tell him then that we were going from one war to another? That it was stupid? If only...

Even when I tried to sleep, my circular thoughts would not let me be. The monkey chatter in my head would not shut up. I hated bedtime, I hated baths, I had trouble sleeping. I quit masturbating in mid-stride and rolled over. The drone of the planes taking off from nearby Hopkins Airport wasn't helping any. I hatched this wild idea about applying to colleges in Canada and eloping with Millie. Maybe to a fairy tale place like Prince Edward Island. I had seen an ad for a university there in the CSU Student Union.

Cutting all my classes the next day, I took the train to Millie to tell her about Prince Edward Island. She was wild about it. Her excitement stunned me. I wrote to the school and mailed the letter the same day, I also wrote to the University of Manitoba, where they had a running ad for someone to teach Hungarian as a third language to Jewish rabbinical students. I thought Millie was seeing right through me. I was trying to evade the draft. Attila the Great was a draft dodger. "You don't think I'm a coward, do you?"

"No!" She kissed me. "Why? Because you love me and want to take me with you?"

She did have a question. How was I going to pay for Prince Edward Island. "You didn't think about that, did you?"

Kinda. As a last resort, I'd have to go begging to my mother and tap into the medical school account. I hated to do it, but what the hey!

Money.

The best things in life were free but what I needed now was money. *My* money. Hell, I worked for it, didn't I? CSU canceled my soccer scholarship. Paying for a second semester was going to be a bitch. As pain in the ass as it was I had no choice but to ask my mother for the money. It didn't surprise me that my heart symptoms were back. And with a vengeance. Goddamm palpitations! Maybe that would be enough to keep me out of the Army. I made an appointment with Dr. Hellerstein, the heart specialist who had been pretty nice to me. Maybe he could write a letter or something to keep me out of the draft. The doc seemed to be on my side.

Millie went with me to University Hospitals, where I was to undergo a battery of tests, including riding a stationary bicycle while technicians monitored my heart and everything.

After a few days the verdict was in: I had enough adrenaline to qualify me for the U.S. Army. Because of my great adrenaline levels my reflexes were better than normal, my freaking nervous system was an asset, not a liability. I had an excellent heart. The heart of a warrior.

Poet and warrior. The sensitivity of a poet, the fierceness of a warrior. How weird was that? Like the character of Steppenwolf in the *Cliffs Notes* I was reading. Light and dark. The guy longing for beauty was the same freaking guy howling like a wolf of the steppes. Like father, like son. Dog shit.

When I told my father I needed money, he was suspicious as shit right off the bat. "I know what it's for," he said. "An abortion."

"God Almighty. No. You always have to say shit like that, don't you? I'm not even going with anybody."

"You're never home. Where are you all that time? You only come home to sleep."

"It so happens I'm hanging out at this pre-Med fraternity called Ars Medica." If my old man knew the real story about me being a father, my *arse* would be grass. I wouldn't have to wait for the Vietcong.

"Fraternity? They should call it Paternity." My old man's words were dripping with his usual sarcasm. "Don't you think I know what fraternities are? Beerhalls and brothels all in one."

"Hah!" I said. "You should know. You were a bohemian."

He was already reaching for a cigarette. "Where did you hear that?"

"When you and your college friend got bombed and reminisced, remember? About how you were so broke you had to cover yourself with a swastika rug."

My father threw his hands in the air. "I give up," he said. "What in the sweet hell is wrong with you? You got your ass kicked out of school, didn't you? That's what it is."

"No, that's not it. My soccer scholarship was for half a year only." This was only a half-truth. I didn't tell him I was cut from the team. "I need money to register for the second half. In fact I need all of my money. I'm not sure about being a doctor."

"Not sure? You better be sure, goddammit! You have any idea how hard your mother and I work to make sure you and your brother get an education. You're about to throw everything to the four winds, aren't you? I may have thrown out some useless furniture in my college days, but I don't remember throwing away my education. Apparently your part-time job, soccer, this fraternity bullshit, and gallivanting around are more important than your books. As for money, you'll have to talk to your mother. You'll find she feels the same way I do. Education comes first. Medical school. A medical doctor is impervious to the whims of regimes. I told you that. You won't see them shipped off to the jungles for cannon fodder."

I felt psyched enough to unfurl my Canadian plan. A mistake. It led to a fierce argument about deserting my family, my religion, and now my adopted country. "For what?" my father blurted. "Don't you think I know what the hell is going on? You're trying to pull a fast one on us, boy. Be very careful. That's all I got to say. If I were you, I'd be very careful."

"I'll just go to Vietnam then." I whipped out the results of my physical and shoved it in his face. "Fit for service it says. Says here I got the heart of a warrior."

"They should've examined your head."

I called him the original escapist if there ever was one. If he was so hung up about America being a Jewish country, why did he bring his goddamm family here in the first place? I was calling the old man's bluff. Were we really fighting the Communists in Southeast Asia, or were we fighting for the interests of Dow Chemical, and so on and so forth?

It went on like this until my mother came home, too exhausted to make dinner. My father heated up some left-over paprikash. When I brought up the matter of the money, my mother turned as white as her hairdresser's uniform. The paprikash got stuck in her throat.

There was no money. My mother had lent my savings to my Uncle Arthúr. Only for a year, she said. My uncle would pay it back with interest. High interest. My Uncle Arthúr was starting up a vault business. Burial vaults. The vaults would be made of fiberglass. Spun glass made of glass fibers and resin. We were all going to be rich, my mother said. It was a sure thing.

My father shot up from the table, his eyes blazing. "Goddamm in heaven! You mean to tell me you sacrificed our sons' future for one of your brother-in-law's scams? Please tell me you didn't!"

"So he misses a year of school. It's not like he's on the Dean's List now, is it?"

"Call that goddamm shyster right now and get the money back. He's a lot better off than we are, and we're lending *him* money! What are we, Chase Manhattan? Call him up now. The boy needs to register."

My mother said she was too tired to argue. She worked all day. Someone had to work around here, she said.

Now it was my turn: "What about all my paychecks?"

She said I was not in medical school yet. That was the deal.

My father said to my mother. "I'm sick and tired of your god-damm brother-in-law. When you bake something, he always ends up with the best piece. Don't you think I have eyes? He's a low-life and a chicken thief! You know what I think? I think he picked the pocket of that poor bastard on the border. And that's just for starters. I know for a fact that Arthúr burned his own place down for the insurance money."

"And where did you hear that?"

"Anna told me."

"Oh, that whore! I should've known," my mother said. "I'm going to bed."

"Oh my God," I bellowed. "Forget Uncle Arthúr for a second. What about me?!"

My mother looked at me and smiled. "You think I'd give you money so you can shack up with that, that Jewess? You better think twice."

"She's a goddamm Catholic. Like you, mother!"

My mother swept her dish of paprikash off the table. The dish shattered on the floor and made a mess. She left it. Marched to bed and slammed the door behind her.

I picked up the broken pieces by hand. There was that image again. Glass. Shattering. Cutting edges. I tried to get the rest up with the broom, but all I did was smear paprikash shit all over the floor. Bitch! I hurled the goddamm broom against the wall.

In the morning my mother announced she and János were going for an extended visit to Hungary as soon as János finished his term at Ohio State. My father and me would simply have to manage without her. If we didn't like the way she was handling the money we were welcome to try it ourselves. Case closed.

"But," my father said.

The case was closed.

My father said if she went back to Hungary, she was never going to see him again.

She went. She didn't wait for János to finish his term. They took a KLM flight to Budapest. They were going to visit relatives and find a suitable Hungarian wife for János. He and a girl in Kecskemét, a town named after goats, were already exchanging letters.

My father told me not to worry. He was going to get the money from Uncle Arthúr. "Your old man has a few tricks up his sleeve."

I was surprised my old man didn't cave in during my mother's absence, at least not on the first day, thanks to his doubling the dose of his anti-depressant. A glass of wine here and there didn't hurt, either. He was all serious about keeping to his schedule of heavy reading and light gardening.

I heard him laugh out loud one morning when he walked into the bathroom to shave. He shaved twice a day for a few days, once at 7 in the morning and again right before noon. He'd put on his bathrobe with these velour lapels. He'd search out "Rákóczy's March" from among the tattered albums wedged under the magazine rack, slide out the record from its dust jacket and flip it on.

His mood was A1. He was in and out of the bathroom as he worked up a good lather in his mug. I saw him apply shaving cream while he hummed to "Rákóczy's March," now and then grimacing to stretch the skin for his straight razor.

The old man was in the groove. I watched as he leaned his face close to the mirror to inspect how close he had gotten. Close. He winked at himself and walked into the living room in invigorated strides. After switching on his reading lamp, he settled into his recliner. He put on his Coca-Cola reading glasses and fooled with a stack of papers he kept in a box. "Attila," he said. "Bring me that bottle of Rosé from under the sink."

I told him he shouldn't be drinking with all those drugs.

"Medicine," he corrected. "I don't do drugs. Kids do drugs. Come here, I want to talk to you."

I put the bottle on the coffee table, next to his new copy of *None Dare Call It Treason*. He didn't read English but he heard about it and just had to have it.

"There's only one way to convince this shyster uncle of yours," my father said. He waved a piece of paper in the air, then nodded and snorted. He lit a cigarette. The tip of his cigarette flamed for a fraction of a second. He inhaled and blew smoke out through his nostrils. "Courtroom testimony. Dated 1945."

"So?"

My father proceeded to tell me Uncle Arthúr had his own skeletons. There were 2000 of them. Near the end of World War II, the man ordered the execution of 2000 Hungarian Jews during a forced march westward. In the Hungarian town of Balf. "Adolf Eichmann," my father said, "had 200,000 killed. Your uncle's share was a neat ten per cent. How 'bout that for a tidy number? The New York Jewish Refugee Aid Society even erected a memorial in Balf. Sure, Arthúr served time in Csillag prison for petty things like forced abortions and deportations, but he was never tried for war crimes. For murder. For extermination. Maybe Simon Wiesenthal and his Nazi Hunters would be interested in a secret little dossier? What do you think?"

"You're actually asking me what I think. I think you're crazy. What about your own skeletons. The Rosenbergs, remember?"

My father's chest started to heave. I thought it was going to explode. But he kept pitching his conspiracy theory about Uncle Arthúr. "Maybe your old man should send them a copy, eh?" He retrieved a sheet of carbon paper, which he held up to the light."

"I don't think Uncle Arthúr burnt down his own place," I said. "The cops ruled it an accident."

"That's convenient. Don't you think I know about rulings. I'm a *Juris Doctor!*"

"And I'm going," I said. "I have a game." But I couldn't escape that easily. There was no end to my old man's diatribe. He was saying that this time Dr. Arthúr Kun is going to pay, and pay big. My old man wasn't asking for much, just enough to put his sons through medical school. A university education was a fortune in America, not to mention an M.D. His sons were worth it.

"Rákóczy's March" played itself out to the scratch of the needle when I left the house.

I was spending almost all of my time with Millie now. She was the only ray of light in the darkening chaos that was my life. I didn't tell her about having no money and that my mother flew the coup to Hungary. I just didn't have the heart. I didn't know how to take my mother's departure. I was angry as shit my mother could just pick up and leave, and envious of the frigging bond between her and my brother. They went all the way back to World War II. When she carried my infant brother on her back like a papoose when they were on the run from the Russians. It was like their skins had melded together. I heard the story more often than I wanted to.

János was like an extension of her. I didn't know where one began and the other ended. My brother did everything, but *everything* my mother wanted. They liked the same foods, the same clothes, the same political parties, shared the same opinions, etc., etc. János was my mother's personal go-fer. Did her shopping at the West Side market, acted as her personal chauffeur, her guard dog. When our parents' fights got physical, János was quick to jump to her aid, and once he even jumped on my father's back to keep him from chasing down my mother. Oh yeah, there was one more thing. János looked a lot more like her side of the family.

The first few days after they left, I felt a surge of freedom. Like a high. But after that, I went down and kept spiraling down until I crashed into a dark well I couldn't climb out of. I had this one dream where I had fallen into one of those deep pole wells in the old village. My mother had thrown me down the well because she didn't want me. She wanted a girl. I'm four years old in the dream. I'm yelling for my mother, but she doesn't hear me. Doesn't or won't. My cries turn into a serenade like in an opera or something but even that isn't enough. I'm rolling my *r*'s so they sounded pretty, like the *r*'s in pu*rr* and se*r*enade, but it still isn't enough. Nothing is enough. She has hardened her heart. She and my brother have a freaking ticket to ride. And they don't care.

I wasn't pissed anymore, just bummed out. Bummed out that her son let her down by doing so poorly in school, that he was turning out to be such a freaking disappointment. That he made her go away.

I felt wiped out, and instead of my usual insomnia I was sleeping all the time. Except when I was with Millie, and that one time I attended a peace rally at school. It beat going to classes. Students and professors arm in arm blowing off school and blowing off steam. Our cause was peace. Our concern was to bring the boys home from Vietnam. One poster read: THE RICH GET RICHER, THE POOR GET KILLED. Another: MILLIONAIRES PROFIT FROM G.I. BLOOD. And: WHAT IF THEY GAVE A WAR AND NOBODY CAME? I was fired up, only to end up having to fight off this anxiety that seemed to have come out of nowhere. Echoes of the first day of protests with my godmother in Budapest. Crazy. After the peace rally I chugged a few bottles of beer at Fat Glenn's and retreated to the war brewing inside me. I tried calling Millie at her dorm but she wasn't in. Where the hell was she? I called Gypsy next. He sounded down, but he came by Fat Glenn's anyway. We polished off I don't know how many bottles of the 3.2 beer. Schlitz or some shit like that. Gypsy said the arson case against him was closed. He was no longer under suspicion. In fact, he was no longer a person of interest.

"Great!" I said.

"Yeah."

"I knew you had nothing to do with it. From day one. I figured they suspected you because of motive or some shit like that. You know how your brother badmouthed my uncle and all that. I swear I didn't say nothing to nobody. I swear it, man! My freaking uncle or some racist shit needed a scapegoat, that's what it is. Anyway, that's my theory. Heck, no way could you do something like that!"

"You think I'm too stupid, don't you?!"

"Jesus, Gypsy, man! That's not what I meant. You told me yourself the cops ruled it an accident!"

"Forget it, man."

We cooled it. Didn't say anything, just drank more beer. We ended up throwing up in the gravel parking lot. I tried talking Gypsy into driving by Millie's Art School, but he just said, "Naw, man."

Gypsy drove erratically. Somehow we made it to my house without totaling the Fastback. My hangover seemed to go on into the next day, and the day after that. I stopped shaving and after a few days sprouted what looked like the beginnings of a goatee.

When Millie saw it she said she liked it. She said I was so handsome. Her hippie. I was sitting on the grass with her one afternoon, stroking the strands of my new goatee, my brooding eyes fixed on the peace sign dangling from a leather string around her neck. I told her I wasn't nuts about it. I wanted to see the necklace with the ivory heart. Where was that?

"At the dorm." She fingered her peace sign. "I've been putting up anti-war flyers most of the day. You don't want to get drafted, do you?"

I made a face.

"What's wrong?"

"I'm not going anywhere. I have Hodgkins Disease," I said.

She did a double take. "What?? Who told you that?"

"I have all the symptoms."

"Like what?"

"Swollen neck glands. Tiredness. Malaise."

"Oh God, Attila, you've got to stop reading that godawful medical book."

It was true. I was reading from the book of torture again. There it was in black and white, the pages spread out in front of me. I'd been feverishly pouring over them for days. No, weeks. "I'm serious." I had her feel the node on the side of my neck.

She said it was nothing. She had that, too. Everybody had it. "You're becoming a hypochondriac."

I didn't say anything.

"What's wrong? Something's wrong," she said.

"I don't know. Everything seems like such a lost cause. I feel like I'm a…loser. I feel like I'd make a shitty father," I said.

A little bug was crawling over the page. I prodded it with a blade of grass as I talked. "I feel I've let everybody down."

"You didn't let me down."

"Yeah, I did. I feel I did. I should've taken you out of here a long time ago. You had to go through all that shit alone. Where was I? I know you called me by the way. My stupid old man had our number changed for the umpteenth time. I don't deserve you. I shouldn't have left your house. I should've stood up to your father then. I shouldn't have let you push me away."

"You enjoy kicking yourself around, don't you?"

"It's not that. It's just that your parents were right. You would've been better off with someone older. More mature. Someone with money and experience. Someone with a real job. Someone who would take care of you the way you deserve to be taken care of. Someone who was taller. Someone like…your father." The pain must've been pretty obvious on my face. I hated myself for being a homeboy. "I don't know, Millie. I don't know what to do!"

"What would you like to do?"

I snorted. I never really thought about it. It was always what I should do. The career my parents mapped out for me. I was supposed to become a doc so I could be impervious to the whims of regimes. My old man's argument sounded not only corny but just as crazy as he was acting lately.

Millie was right. I was a hypochondriac. With enough knowledge to torment myself by scaring myself to death. For me an M.D. would be a "terminal" degree. "You know, you're right," I said to Millie. "I *am* a hypochondriac. I'm just lugging this freaking book around to please my old man." I slammed the book shut and handed it to her. "Feel how heavy it is."

Millie weighed the telephone-size book. "Holy Moses," she said. "Feels like a ton of bricks."

I took the book from her, whipped it open to show her what bullshit gobbledygook it was. That's when I noticed the squashed bug on the page. The splattered brown body looked like a freaking Rosarch.

We burst out laughing. It was a sign.

"What do you make of it?" asked Millie.

I scrutinized the symmetrical image from different angles. "What I see here is two people making out. They're celebrating. This shitty little bug just saved them 11 years of bullshit. God, I feel lighter already."

Millie's eyes lit up. She was happy for me. We kissed. We laughed like crazy. We had squashed the bug.

"No more medical school," I said. "Screw medical school."

"Screw medical school," she said.

I jumped up, walked to the water's edge, wound up like for a hammer throw and hurled the stinking book, bug and all, into the lagoon. The splash was like the parting of the Red Sea. Millie clapped. She was standing, giving me a standing ovation.

We settled back on the grass. God, I felt good in my skin. I lit a cigarette, lay back so my head was in Millie's lap. She was playing with my hair. I was blowing smoke rings in the air and watched them sail off into the blue. She had me close my eyes and drew lazy circles around my lips. I pushed my tongue out to kiss her finger. I heard her swallow and opened my eyes. I could see her mouth. I tossed away my cigarette unfinished.

"I know what you want," she said.

I wanted to stay with her on the grass here by the lagoon and do nothing but write poetry to her. I brought her face down for a kiss. "I want you," I said.

"I love you," she said and kissed me back.

I was on another cigarette when she asked me what I thought I might like to do. In life.

"I don't know. Poetry?"

"You can always change your major to English, you know."

"Naw. What would I do with English?"

"Lots of things. You could teach. Write poetry on the side. Stories. You have a pretty wild imagination."

I gave her a twisted grin. "Teach?" Teaching was not exactly my bag. I had to laugh at the insanity of a foreigner teaching Americans their own language. And poetry? I always felt my words didn't match my thoughts. Once I wrote them down, they sounded hollow and stupid. It was a struggle just to make sense. With English as my second language, it would be like a blind man trying to be a dentist. For me, poetry could never become a career or a hobby. I wrote because I had to, not because I wanted to. I had to wrestle with every word. Hand-to-hand combat was more like it.

Millie thought the poems were about her. Or was there someone else? she kidded me.

"No!" My forceful denial bugged the shit out of me, and I had no idea why. Honestly.

CHAPTER 10

"Tonight I summon the barbarian to my bed
you without conscience or hope
without limit or regret
with the torch of the phallus
in your eyes
with the world's sour sweat on your limbs
with the wombs of all women
in your hands
with a conqueror's sword
in your thighs
fire for fire, lust for lust
Tonight I want you
demon and no man to be."

—Lili Bita, "The Barbarian"

A week later, Millie sneaked me into her dorm room. She had a surprise for me: a portrait of herself taken in the same light blue dress and the ivory heart necklace she wore when we exchanged vows. There was more. She had picked up a sexy nightgown at Higbee's. Holy shit! I thought. I tried grabbing her right then and there, but she pushed me away. Gently. There was to be no hanky-panky in the Agnes Gund House. But she did have reservations for us at the Commodore Hotel in Little Italy. She said we could finally spend the whole night in a bed like decent people, and not have to slink around in the great outdoors like alley cats, or risk getting spied on by peeping toms. The hotel had a shower and everything, which was great, and I could have her as many times as I wanted. Oh, there was one more thing. She got her period. And was over it.

I was instantly hyper about doing an all-nighter with Millie. I phoned my father from the hotel lobby. I was breathless when I told him our bus broke down just outside of Columbus, that the college was putting the team up in a hotel. Should be back in Cleveland the next day. Anyway, our team won 3 to 2 in overtime.

I gave Millie the OK sign after I hung up. Everything was all set. My father said my Uncle Arthúr's was on his way over with the money, but I didn't want to let the cat out of the bag just yet and said nothing to Millie. A hundred million things could go wrong. Instead, I said, "Shit! If only my old man knew I tossed his freaking book down the waters of Lethe!"

"I'm glad you did. Don't you feel better?"

Oh yeah, I nodded.

The hotel lobby was a combo restaurant and pharmacy, smelling of bacon and cigar smoke, with Beeman's chewing gum thrown into the mix.

Millie went up to the room first. She told me to browse by the magazine rack a bit before I came up. *Time* magazine's April cover was pretty mind-blowing: IS GOD DEAD? I leafed through it in seconds. My mind was on something else. I gave the waiting game another minute, maybe less, and hurried up to the fourth floor and room 421. It added up to 7, Millie's lucky number.

She opened the door in a red paisley, satin gown, with a slit on the side that ran from the floor to her hip. Her nipples floated easily under the smooth fabric. I took a deep breath. She was knock-out gorgeous.

"Happy anniversary," she said. She tried handing me a greeting card in a pink envelope, but I was too busy holding her by the waist, pressing her to me and nibbling on her neck. "You read it to me," I said between kisses.

She read the greeting card poem out loud.

"Beautiful," I said.

"You don't like it. The poem, I mean. Don't blame you. Your poetry is so much better." She kissed me. "See, that's another thing you could do with your poetry. How would you like to work for a place like American Greeting? Writing poems all day. Huh? No?" Another kiss. "What would you like to do?"

"I want to make love to you."

"You do, huh?"

She made sure the door was locked and chained.

I lifted her off the floor and carried her to the bed. I took my time this time. I mean I really took my time. I touched her, I ran my hands over her satin nightgown. I was exploring her body, her long legs, her calves, the hollow at the back of her knee, the curve of her hips, her side, the smooth inside of her arms, kissing her everywhere, not leaving anything untouched. Kissing her behind the ear tickled her. I did her neck and back. She said she liked that, liked her back massaged. I gave her the royal treatment, so to speak. "Yes, yes," she cooed. "There. Ahh." It was heaven.

We took our time making love. While we held each other afterwards, every cell in my body felt this easy, limber, incredible glow. We lay there sleepy and content. I lit a cigarette, took a deep, satisfying drag and blew smoke toward the ceiling. I was never so mellow as I was at that moment. Never.

After I finished the cigarette, I wanted her again. We took a shower just so we could do it in the shower. I got a charge out of soaping up her breasts and sliding my hands all over her body. I washed her back. I turned her around so I could do her breasts again. I did them separately, devoting equal attention to each breast. Then I did them together. I slid my hand between her legs. She liked it. I had her soapy body pinned against the ceramic tile when I entered her. I was hard, and she told me.

We toweled each other off and went back to bed. I was kissing her belly softly when she said, "Can you be a little rougher?"

I stopped. "What do you mean?"

"You know, just a little rougher?"

Rougher? I thought. What did that mean? I tried grabbing her shoulders roughly but I was afraid I might hurt her. It was awkward. Very awkward. My heart wasn't in it. I was losing heart. And I was losing my hard.

Millie caught on and said she was just kidding.

"No you weren't."

"Yes, I was. Come on."

She took her pillow and whacked me on the head with it and burst out laughing. The tension was broken. We had the sillies. Pillow fight, the whole bit. One pillow burst and there were feathers everywhere.

I was doing the twist in the raw. She said it was funny the way my dingaling moved.

"Look at *you*," she laughed. She couldn't stop. She was red in the face. She doubled over.

Our new-found freedom made us play like crazed puppies. A hickey or two in private places. We did all the things we couldn't do outside. It was a workout. "Whew," Millie said. She was pooped. And famished. "Oh-kay," she said. "Let's get dressed. We're going out."

Off we went to a restaurant on Murray Hill in Little Italy. Millie's idea. She was footing the bill. Or, rather, her father was.

Halfway up Murray Hill was a cute little Italian place called Guarino's. Ivy and arched windows and little white statues and all that. Millie felt obliged to buy the expensive bottle of Italian Chianti on the table. I guess she looked sophisticated enough to buy booze without having to flash an ID. The strong wine on our empty stomachs gave us an immediate buzz. The sillies continued. For starters, Millie ordered shrimp cocktail.

Shrimp was a problem for me, and I said so. "My mother said shrimp reminded her of rooster dicks," I told Millie.

Millie couldn't stop laughing. She held up a shrimp and said they were pretty small. "More like little boy dicks? I never saw rooster dicks. Wait a minute I never saw any roosters. Live, I mean. I mean a real rooster. You know what I mean."

We kept sipping the Chianti and laughing and going nuts.

"Must've been eons ago," Millie laughed, "that your mother saw yours."

"Guess so."

"Oh God," Millie said suddenly. "I'm drunk."

"Eat some more of those rooster dicks. You'll feel better."

"They're not rooster dicks, they're little boy dicks. What do you call these in Hungarian?"

"We don't have shrimp."

"No, you crazy man. I don't mean shrimp. I mean, you know what I mean?"

"*Pilinkó.*"

"Say it again."

I repeated it.

I couldn't say why, but I started to feel uncomfortable. I don't know, it didn't feel right. Maybe it was that one word, *Pilinkó*. I used to hear it all the time when I first moved in with my godparents. In those day I called them godmother and godfather. My godmother was obsessed about having me run around naked. I guess I didn't mind because I remember shrieking as I ran around the couch. "I'm going to catch you," she was chasing and teasing me. "I'm going to catch you." Then my godfather ambushed me out of nowhere. "What have got there now? A fancy horn have we?" "It's not a horn," my godmother said. "Tell your godfather what you have there. "My *Pilinkó*," I shouted with glee. I guess they liked me parading around with my *Pilinkó* out. I can't say the same thing for my mother. She hated my nakedness. When I wasn't decent, she got into the habit of saying the pussy cat was on the prowl looking for naked little boys. "She'll bite it right off, she will. Where's Kitty? Here Kitty-kitty-kitty. Where is that pussy cat?"

Our waiter returned to take our order for the main course. Millie told him to bring out more appetizers. More *Pilinkós*. She held up her empty bowl of shrimp. She laughed so hard she had to catch her breath. She leaned close to me and whispered, "Oh God, you know what? I saw my father's, what did you call it again, *Pilin-goat??*" She was laughing like a maniac. "A day or two before we got caught. Let's see. The day before. God. Did I tell you this? A day or two before we got caught, I hear some knocking against my wall. You know? I was scared and I didn't know what it was. So, I go into my parents' room, right? And see my Dad making love to my mom." Millie's hand went to her mouth. "You think he stopped? You think my father stopped? Not on your life. He gave me a dirty look and kept on going."

"And your mother?"

"She just lay there like a log. Oblivious to it all."

"So, when did you see his—?"

"*Pilin-goat??*"

"It's *Pilinkó*."

"Whatever. Did anyone ever tell you you're a pervert?" Another giggle from Millie. "Oh God. Afterwards. When he went to the bathroom. All he had on was a T-shirt."

I was stunned. Drunk as I was, I was stunned. Probably more than I should've been. So much for the illusion of the wholesome American family. All I could say to Millie was—

I didn't know what to say to Millie. So I asked: "Why didn't you tell them they broke *your* heart?"

"I'm sure. Be serious."

I told her I was. "You said you had a breakdown because you thought you broke their hearts. What about *your* heart?"

Millie wasn't laughing any more. She was crying. By the time her second order of shrimp arrived, she lost her appetite. I had to help her make out the check. When she got up from the table she was dizzy, said "whoa" and I had to hold on to her while we stumbled out of Guarino's, onto the wet pavement and flickering neon. The little white statues in the arches were lit an eerie color of green.

Shit. Shit. Shit. I was sorry for wrecking Millie's rare mood. Now she was really strung out. I was going to have to cheer her up so we could continue where we left off. But in my heart of hearts, I knew something had happened. Something that could not be undone.

By the time I got her back to our hotel room she was dead to the world and just lay there like a log, exactly the way she had described her mother.

Blue light from the television washed over Millie's body. I caressed her even though she was dead to my touch. I couldn't sleep. I watched her breathe and remembered watching my mother and then my godmother breathe when I was a little kid. Always afraid they would stop breathing as soon as I stopped watching. Tonight was no different. I kept an all night vigil, getting up for an occasional cigarette and to write down some lines of poetry that wouldn't let me be unless I wrote them down.

With the first light of dawn, I looked out the window to see the outlines of an inner courtyard. There was a spiral fire escape. It was like *déjà vu*. I was looking out into the courtyard of my godmother's apartment in Budapest. The same spiral staircase that led all the way down to the bowels of the earth.

The checkbook with Millie's and her Dad's name printed on top lay on the table next to her Dad's condom wrappers, the tin foil turned inside out. There was that same sick rubber smell. Suddenly I felt like there wasn't enough air in the room. Like I was going to get sick from all the goddamm shrimp. It wasn't agreeing with me. I felt hot and cold. I was probably allergic to the damned shrimp.

I moved the table and tried to open the window. Impossible. The cheap paint had glued it shut. It hadn't been opened in years. The effort made me breathless. I felt like I was suffocating. A cold, sick feeling rumbled through my body, my heart was pounding, beating up on me from the inside.

Millie looked like she was coming to, moaning, stretching like a cat. But then she rolled over on her side. The folds on her satin nightgown were like waves in a red sea of Chianti. And I was drowning in it. All that booze was making me sick to my stomach.

She no longer smelled of Christmas spice. She smelled like rubbers, too. I went to the bathroom. I had the dry heaves. Finally I threw up. It was all that shrimp and all that goddamn Chianti. I didn't get to sleep a wink, not a frigging wink. I did finish the poem which I titled "Angina." I finished it before Millie woke up. It was not something I would be able to show her. Closing the lid on the toilet I sat down, lit a cigarette and read some of the lines over and over again through the eye-stinging smoke:

> *You ride me with great art*
> *You ride me like a teeter-totter*
> *Into your vagina*
> *Into your womb you ride my heart*

Not exactly the stuff of greeting card poetry.

My forehead tightened. I looked at my watch. Already eleven. Jesus. I told my old man I'd be home by noon.

I rushed Millie to get dressed. My irritation didn't escape her. She said she had a wallbanger of a headache. "Can we just slow down a little bit. I need some coffee. Can't you call him again? Say you were delayed?"

I hesitated. Okay. Okay. I telephoned him from the room, telling him I wouldn't be home till later in the evening. Our last goal, I said, ended up being disqualified because one of our players turned out to be a professional from Argentina. Against NCAA rules. Now we had to play in a playoff. Nuts.

My father told me I was doing an admirable job narrating a game that never took place. "Come on, son. It's your father you're talking to. You left your soccer spikes behind! Wouldn't playing barefoot be against your NCAA rules? Just a question."

I was busted. What was there left to say? I had to be quick on my feet to come up with another lie.

"Why don't you just come home, son?"

"The team provides extra pairs. Kids forget their spikes all the time. The one they gave me is a crappy fit. Real crap. Maybe that's why I stank. Hello?"

"I'm here. Alright, son."

I wasn't hungry but Millie enjoyed a leisurely brunch of a BLT sandwich and French fries. We split a large orange juice and strolled around the Italian neighborhood until Millie spotted Holy Rosary Church. She wanted us to go in. Since she'd been away from home she's been coming to this little Italian church. It always made her feel better.

Millie had to pull my arm.

"Alright, alright already," I said. I was desperate to feel better, but church was the last place where I wanted to be. I just needed to throw up. Was it the juice that was making me feel queasy? Cool perspiration burst all over my body.

Holy Rosary was an old church, like the ones in Hungary. It was a strange morning. Everything was eerily familiar. But it was more than that. The church was empty and its emptiness frightened me. I was certain something terrible was going to happen. I could barely control my breathing and, as insane as it was, I wondered if Millie could see my heart pounding through my shirt. She was leading me to the side altar where she knelt before a statue of the Virgin Mary. I stood by dumbly. Mary looked so chaste in her light blue mantle and wreath of spring flowers. Like the flowers the kids would pick for the

Virgin, singing songs like, "O Mary, We Crown Thee With Garlands Today." My father called all this the "cult" of Mary. A holdover from man's pagan past, he'd say. God just had to have a mother. A God-Mother. Except not all godmothers were perfect.

I did not kneel down in front of Mary. I was trying to slow my breathing. It wasn't working. Fear was giving way to anger. Christ. Shouldn't we have first gone to the main altar, genuflected and crossed ourselves? What was more important? God the Father? Or the Holy Mother? *Jézus Krisztus!* The monkey chatter in my head was back and with a vengeance. Here I was in God's house sounding like a fucking ape. The fucking monkey brain would not shut up! It was sacrilege. I was downright wicked, and I was breaking my father's heart as Millie broke God the Father's heart. That thing about her father in nothing but a T-shirt. It was my sin, too. I was living in sin, and by living in sin I was breaking God the Father's heart.

I blew air out. Slowly.

Millie whispered that on Saturdays the priest heard confessions. I nodded mechanically, my heart still in my throat.

There were no lines. We entered the Gothic confessional booth from either side.

I opened the confessional door, and in the half-dark saw the red velvet kneeler and the screen. The priest was an ominous shadow behind it.

My turn came first.

I kneeled, crossed myself, and took a deep breath. "Bless me, Father, for I have sinned." I waited till a count of five before I said, "I used the name of God in vain."

"What else?"

"I've had sex, Father. In a hotel. With…my wife."

There was something that sounded like a cough on the other side of the screen.

"The thing is…Millie and me, we performed the ceremony, I mean the marriage ceremony, by…ah…ourselves. In the Valley."

The priest sighed, "How many times?" in a heavy Italian accent.
I didn't answer.
"How many times did you fornicate?"
I still said nothing.
"How many times did you have sex with the woman in the hotel?"
"Ah, four or five."
"What did you do, go on a spree? No, no, no, my son. This will never do. You must tell her a marriage like that is invalid in the eyes of Mother Church. Do you understand?"
"She was just 17. It's my—"
I heard a gasp from the other side of the confessional.
It was Millie.
"You bastard!" She whipped open my door and screamed at me. Was that what I thought of our marriage?
Sobbing, she tore the ivory heart from her neck and threw it at me in the darkness. Then she ran out of the church.

I found myself walking around Little Italy in a daze. Must've been for hours. I had to keep walking, keep the blood moving. I was afraid if I'd stop, I'd burst out crying like a little boy or I'd throw up. Had to keep moving, had to keep telling myself I was 18. Old enough to die in a jungle in Vietnam. I took the steep climb up Mayfield Road, alongside Lake Cemetery, where I once played ball among statues of winged angels with broken noses. It seemed like another lifetime ago.
By the time I boarded the train home it was pretty late. I rode in numb silence one stop shy of the end of the line where I usually caught a connecting bus. I remember stepping off the train one moment, and being on the tracks the next. It was all insanely impulsive. All of a sudden, I found myself on the tracks below. I heard the wheels grind and I saw the lights. I had just enough time to hop over the tracks and hoist myself up onto the eastbound platform to avoid being run over. In the process, I got some oil or tar shit on my shirt.

Otherwise, I was fine. Once I caught my breath, I realized I must've jumped off the westbound platform and was now on the platform heading east, back toward Millie. Something in me would not let her go. I lit a cigarette, only to toss it. The eastbound train was about to close its doors and head out.

I was on the right track to get Millie back. When I got off at University Circle, the shuttle bus had stopped running. I quickened my pace up Murray Hill to Holy Rosary Church.

The heavy brown doors were chained and bolted.

I jogged down the hill, raced across Euclid Avenue by the Commodore and cut through a bunch of athletic fields, and slowed down only when I got on the sidewalk of the girls' dorms. The Agnes Gund House doors were bolted, too, maybe one light on in the whole damned building. I walked under a street lamp to check my watch. 1:50 a.m. The trains had quit running. I swore and gave the hedges a kick. I had no other choice but to walk back to the Commodore and call my father. He sounded groggy. I explained I was…delayed.

"What time is it? Where are you?"

"I'm at this hotel called the Commodore."

"Hotel?"

"Yeah. One of our players works the night-shift here. In the restaurant. He's supposed to give me a ride home."

My father said I didn't sound like myself. Was I tired? My father yawned. "Where are you exactly?"

"Around the old high school."

"What?! Cathedral Latin? You're way over there in niggertown? At this time of the night? Jesus Christ. This soccer business has to stop. This is nonsense. Nonsense. I'll pick you up."

I'd usually have a snappy comeback like he was the one who sent me here to high school—for how many years?—so I could risk my life studying Latin to become a doctor. No snappy reply this time. Just didn't have the energy. I simply said: "No you're not. You are *not* picking me up."

"What's wrong with you? Something's wrong."

"I broke up with Millie. Or she broke up with me."

There was a lull. I could hear my father's wheezing. "Is this the Jew?"

"This is the Jew."

"Can't say your mother and I didn't warn you. She would've been disastrous for you, son. And not only for your career. In their heart of hearts, they're all atheists. They crucified the Christ."

"Fuck you!" I slammed the phone so hard, the clerk at the Commodore said, "Hey! Watch that!"

I sat shivering on a bus bench in front of Severence Hall.

The early morning commute was well on its way when I got up and walked to the Agnes Gund House. Only to find out that Millie didn't sleep there last night or the night before. She had gone home for the weekend.

What I did next was walk to the Rapid station and climb the wire fence, like I used to in my high school days, when I ran out of money, which was often. Once off the train I thumbed the rest of the way and was home by 7:30 a.m.

The trouble was, my father wasn't. The garage door was wide open, but no car. Where was the Chrysler?

I didn't have a house key. Because I always lost my key, my parents stopped providing me one. But I did have a routine. I broke into my own house on a regular basis. Around back through a basement window. I had this way of wriggling through, like I was doing the frigging limbo rock.

I heard the telephone ring non-stop just as I landed on the basement floor. I bounded up the steps, taking them by two's.

It was Anna on the line. She said she didn't want to frighten me, but Fairview Hospital called her to tell her a Ferenc Nagy was in an automobile accident. They called her because her number was the only number in my father's wallet. She told me I should call the hospital.

When I called, a woman who identified herself as a nurse asked me if I was sitting down. I sat down and braced myself. The nurse said my father was dead on arrival when the ambulance brought him in at 3:15 a.m. She was sorry.

I was supposed to call the Fairview Police Department as soon as possible. I did. They told me to come in. They wanted to hand over my father's personal effects and had a few questions.

I walked the four miles to the now familiar police station. Tired, dusty, and stinking, I sat on the other side of a familiar gray metal desk. The Jaycees and presidential photographs were still on the wall, but this time I was staring past them. I found out that Sergeant Lang was no longer with the force. The new Sergeant was Mr. Johnson, the man with the Afro who pulled me out of class. The first thing Sergeant Johnson asked me was, how I was faring.

"Alright."

"Your mother and brother, I understand, are out of the country, so your father's friend told us. You have any way of notifying them? Contacting your mother?"

I thought for a moment, then shook my head no.

"I'm really sorry," the Sergeant said. "I know it must've come as a shock. Things like this, you never know what to say. I was the first one on the scene. On Columbia Road. I called for the ambulance right away. You father hit a tree head-on. His head went through the windshield. When I got to him he was choking on his dentures. I tried prying them out of his mouth, but that wasn't the real problem. The real problem was that your father broke his neck. By the time the ambulance arrived he had expired. There was nothing anyone could've done."

Sergeant Johnson shook his head slowly.

He had a few questions. Was my father depressed lately?

"No."

"Did he ever talk about killing himself?"

"No."

"Did he have a drinking problem?"

"Just wine."

"Did he have any enemies?"

Enemies? I thought. Why?

It was a question the police had to ask. I still didn't get it. What was I supposed to say? The Communists? The Zionists? The Masons? All of the above? There was a car once that swerved out of its way to splash us as we were going to church in our Sunday best. My father was convinced the driver was a Communist out to nail us. And there were the Rosenbergs…

I glanced at Sergeant Johnson's kindly face and told him my father didn't have any enemies.

"Good enough," the Sergeant said. "It looks like your dad lost control of his car. We still have to go over a few things, like blood alcohol levels, things like that. I'm pretty sure it'll all come out okay. You have any questions?"

I didn't. I was numb. Cold and numb.

The Sergeant picked up the phone and asked that Mr. Nagy's personal effects be brought in so his son could sign for them.

I was handed a bulging envelope of my father's belongings. His wallet and whatever he had in his pockets at the time, stuff like that.

I signed my name at the bottom of a printed form.

When the Sergeant asked me if I knew of any funeral homes, I nodded. "Yes, Bodnár & Sons on Lorain Avenue. I have an uncle in the business, also."

"Maybe your uncle can help out."

I didn't tell the Sergeant that since my famous outburst at the Lake Erie League meeting, my uncle and Mr. Bodnár were not exactly friends. Jesus. Maybe something like this would bring them together. "Maybe."

The Sergeant escorted me outside and pointed to the Golden Arches across the street. "May help if you get a bite to eat. A Coke or something. Good luck to you, son." He handed me his card with his number on it. He told me I could call him if I needed to.

I thanked the Sergeant and headed over to the Mac's I was fired from not long ago. I didn't recognize any of the faces. I was flat broke and hoped my father had some money in his wallet. I was starving. I glanced into the brown paper bag. My father's gold-plated watch was wrapped around his wallet. There were green bills inside.

I ordered a fish sandwich and a large Coke. I took my tray to a seat that wasn't facing the brick police station. Should I put the watch on my wrist? No. It wouldn't be right. Wouldn't feel right. There was thirty dollars in the wallet. Anna's name and phone number. And something else. A faded piece of paper, folded, crumbling along the fold. I unraveled it carefully and received another shock. It was my very first poem, written when I was nine years old. About the Hungarian Revolution. A little ten-line thing, a line or two plagiarized from somewhere, but most of it was mine. I was amazed my father carried it in his wallet all this time.

The other item in the bag was a paper towel folded over. My father's broken dentures. The paper was sticking to the plastic roof of the mouth. I looked out the window at the spaces between the trees. I didn't touch my sandwich. I couldn't. I took a few sips from my Coke. My mouth was very dry.

Gypsy drove me to my Uncle Arthúr's farm, but he didn't come in. He waited in the car. The barn, where I found my uncle, had been converted to a mini-factory where he and his team of illegal aliens were pouring fiberglass into a mold. He called his new company the Heritage Vault Corporation. The logo on his letterhead was 14-carat gold. So he said.

News of my father's death barely interrupted his stride. He did pour himself some milk and *pálinka* in a tall glass, more *pálinka* than milk this time. "Does your mother know?"

"No. That's why I'm here. I can't get a hold of her in Hungary. She didn't leave a phone number or anything. Nothing. They're in Kecskemét or some town like that. I phoned you but no one picked up. I guess you were out here working."

My uncle's thick fingers dug into his pocket for a piece of paper. "Let's give it a shot," he said.

"Where are they staying?" I asked.

"Visiting relatives. Probably. I got a number here. Let's see if it works." He downed what was left in his glass. It took some doing, dialing and redialing the eleven digit overseas number before we got through. Miraculously. Uncle Arthúr handled the call. I barely got to speak to my mother and brother. My mother told me to be strong. We all had to be strong. She asked if my father had been drinking. I said I didn't know. Didn't think so. My uncle said it was a tragedy. My mother repeated the word "tragedy" and told me to be strong again. They would take the first available flight back, but it may take a couple of days. "Your uncle's taking care of everything."

"No. I am, mother."

A lopsided smirk from Uncle Arthúr.

Once we hung up, my uncle pulled out a slab of salt pork and onions from the small fridge in the corner and cut us both a healthy slice of bread. "A little *pálinka*?"

I didn't want to drink. I was already light-headed and sweating like crazy. I felt like I had an ice pack on my back. It surprised me that I didn't feel anything, I mean emotionally. I didn't cry. Didn't or couldn't. Only my body reacted. Instead of tension, it was a total slackening of every muscle in my body. Blah. I felt blah. Wound down. It was more physical than anything else. After the police station and McDonald's, I bought these over-the-counter pills called Compoz. A mistake. The two blue pills I gulped down made me queasy. Having pure grain alcohol on top of it wouldn't be too smart. I'd vomit for sure.

"You look like shit," my uncle said. "Eat something."

"I can't right now."

"Can't? How will you take care of everything if you can't?"

"Uncle Arthúr? Did you give the money to my father? The money my mother invested in your business? It was mine. Close to three thousand dollars. And what about Aunt Piroshka's money? The money she gave my mother?"

My uncle laughed as if he just heard the funniest joke of his life. "You are a greenhorn, aren't you? I like your spirit, though. I like your spirit. Let me fill in a few gaps in your education. There are some things you ought to know about your father. One. He was charming in the extreme. Oh, not around the family. But around women. Young women. Women of taste. Expensive women. Our Anna was just a fling. A diversion. But not a cheap date. Had to be the best brandy. Diamond earrings. You get the picture. Who do you think your father was with the night he died? Anna!"

I didn't believe him. My father was about to pick me up the night he died. I knew that much. The stuff about Anna? It didn't make any sense. Just didn't.

My uncle wouldn't leave it alone. "You didn't know that, did you?" he said.

I acted like it was no big thing. Although it was. "No biggie," I said, shrugging it off. "Who isn't screwing Anna?"

"I'm not. I don't have time for foolishness now. I got my fiberglass vault business to think of. It's really going to take off. I mean *really*. I could use someone like you. I just had the Catholic Cemetery Association endorse it. They tested our prototype and we passed with flying colors. The lid is shaped like the hull of a submarine. It's all honeycomb inside. We use epoxy and resin. It's the wave of the future. Concrete vaults are going to become obsolete. Would you want your father to be laid into the ground in a septic tank? That's what those old vaults are like. They're porous. Ours never rusts, leaks or rots. Maybe that could be our motto. What do you think?"

"I'm sorry, Uncle Arthúr, but I'm going to have to use your toilet."

"Can you translate that for me into college English? We'll print up a dummy pamphlet before you go to Bodnár's." He stopped talking when he heard gagging and the toilet flush.

I was back. I made the mistake of imagining my father's body floating around in my uncle's flimsy fiberglass coffin. On *my* money. Sick. I told my uncle I needed the money first, the three thousand, then maybe after that we could talk about how I can help the Heritage Vault Corporation.

My uncle sized me up, smiled. "You're a real piece of work, you know that? That cute little girl has been teaching you a few tricks, hasn't she? Come on, tell me. Hasn't she?"

I told him that actually we broke up.

He was sorry to hear it. She could've been a real asset. And not only her ass.

"I gotta go. Gypsy's waiting."

"Wait," he said. He took out his billfold and pulled out three crisp hundred-dollar bills. "Here's ten per cent. A start, right? Would you at least say something to Bodnár about fiberglass? Tell him it's silver metallic and it's shaped like a submarine hull."

I was on my way out. My uncle was behind me, coaching me how to pitch his frigging fiberglass, walking me to Gypsy's Fastback.

"Tell him it's lightweight, 110 lbs. Even with a dead body it's...You don't need all those goddamm pall bearers," he shouted after me.

I was in the car with the window still down. "Just get me the rest of my money so I can bury my father," I shouted back.

He came up to the car and put his face close enough so I could see the hairs on his nose. In a whisper that was more like a hiss, he said: "Listen to you. You already buried your father. With all your American hogwash. You hated him, remember? You called him old man. Now it's father. Okay. But he's not the Pharaoh. Three thousand is a bit extravagant, don't you think? Have Bodnár give me a call and we'll work something out. Something reasonable. Something your mother can afford. Don't go off hot-headed, full of sanctimonious remorse. You're better off hitting the books. That's what your father would've wanted. And don't tell me it's not."

"Not!" I said. I rolled up the window. I said something to Gypsy, then rolled down the window again and shouted: "What about Chicago?! Life is pretty cheap for you, isn't it?"

"You're on drugs," he raged. "Stupid American shit!"

The window went back up and the Fastback fishtailed out of the driveway, spitting gravel.

Bodnár & Sons Funeral Parlor was in a predominantly Hungarian neighborhood, on the corner of Lorain and Forty-first next to Fisher's grocery store, Kossuth Bookstore, and an empty lot that used to be the bar and grill.

Mr. Bodnár was impeccable in the dark suit he always wore. There were no coffins to look at in the funeral parlor. Mr. Bodnár put me in his shiny black Cadillac and drove me to an old brick warehouse in the seediest section of town. When we stopped, Mr. Bodnár was quick to swing around and open the door for me.

Mr. Bodnár called it the showroom. Row after row of polished coffins. Stage lighting. Candelabras. Plastic flowers. After Mr. Bodnár said, "I'm sure you and your family would want what is best for your papa," he tried selling me the most expensive coffin in the showroom. About the price of his new Cadillac.

"It's beautiful, Mr. Bodnár, but too expensive. We're regular people. My father was not ostentatious." When I thought about it, my father was one of the most ostentatious men I had ever known. Someone who would go out of his way to procure Dunhill cigarettes, sometimes making an extra trip to the airport where they sold them, so he could impress his friends. Though he was unemployed, he had his shirts sent out to be washed and starched, and his suits pressed. After a meticulous shaving ritual, he'd don one of his suits, put on a tie, his gold-plated wrist watch, just to read the Hungarian daily.

Mr. Bodnár poured it on in that solemn, caring way of his. Because he knew our family to be a good Hungarian family, we wouldn't have to pay for the funeral all at once. Mr. Bodnár wanted me to know that I had his personal assurance on that. He said he always thought very highly of my father and my Uncle Arthúr's commitment to Hungarian sport. And he said my uncle's pioneer work with fiberglass vaults was nothing short of amazing. Quite a family. Cleveland was fortunate to have Hungarians like us in the community. It was people like us who made America great.

Embarrassed, I gave up eye contact with Mr. Bodnár. The man was as polished as his coffins.

"I know," Mr. Bodnár said, "this must be very difficult for you. Your mother, I'm sure, is going to be very proud of you for making the arrangements." Mr. Bodnár steepled his hands as we strolled down aisle after aisle of ornate coffins, arranged in some kind of descending order of price and elegance.

We were in the last row when I made my selection. A humble imitation bronze with a price tag that was close to $3000.

My next stop was the florist.

Mr. Gayer was a tall, balding Hungarian-American and friend of the family. He had a pretty wife, Americanized to the point of being an alcoholic. I was shocked when I realized I was already thinking like my father. My father would consider this woman an alcoholic because she drank whiskey, but a Hungarian who drank Blood of the Bull or pure-grain *pálinka* was another story. The family had remarked on a few occasions that Mrs. Gayer overate, overdrank, and overfucked.

Both Mr. and Mrs. Gayer smoked like chimneys. I found them friendly, down to earth. Instead of reciting the usual pat phrase like, "Please accept our deepest sympathies," they said, "Geez, we're sorry, pal. Really." But it didn't stop the Gayers from selling me an overpriced floral cross of red, white and green carnations. Hungarian colors.

I figured I'd pay for it somehow. I could go back to McDonald's and try making it full-time for a while. My father had been proud of being Hungarian, though by blood he wasn't. His family was German, mostly. His father's name was Hoffmann and his mother's Singer. It was all very confusing. My father insisted it wasn't blood that counted but your belief in what you were. Your sensibility. By sensibility, he was Hungarian. Some of the greatest Hungarian poets and warriors may have been of Croatian or Slovakian descent, but by sensibility they were all Hungarian. When I asked if this could be true of Jews, my father said no. Jews were Jews first.

He had refused to allow that Millie was Catholic. It didn't work that way, he said. She would always be a Jew. It was a race, blue eyes or not. She would always choose Jewish concerns over Hungarian concerns. She would always choose her father over me, no matter what kinds of rebellious games she was intent on playing. In the end she would always be his Jewish princess. Always his. It was biblical. The Catholic thing was just a matter of a private school and nothing more. Didn't János and I attend a Catholic high school, although we were Lutherans?

My father was deeply hurt by my change of religion, which he found out just a short time before he died. In one of our many confrontations, he had said, "Anyone who abandons his nationality, his religion, and his family, ceases to be a man. He is nothing. Nothing but a spineless blob of Jello." Like most people in this country. America was not a melting pot, but Jello salad.

Once I left the florist, I realized I hadn't eaten anything since yesterday. On the corner of Lorain and Forty-fifth, there was a little hot dog joint called the Greeks, where they stacked the sweaty wieners in huge pyramids right against the store window. Without thinking about it, I wolfed down three chili dogs.

By overspending on a floral cross of Hungarian colors, I was hoping I would somehow make up for hurting my father. By adjusting to this godless country he and my mother brought me to. The Hungarian cross would be signed, "From Your Devoted Son, Attila."

I felt a chill, a gust of emotion. But I didn't cry. I couldn't. That's why my next stop, at 3:00 a.m. was the emergency ward of Fairview Hospital. I told the first nurse I saw that I was dying.

It was my heart. A terrible tightness, like a noose around my chest. I was short of breath.

The attending doctor ordered a routine EKG, which was normal. My pulse was fast, but it looked more like stress, perhaps indigestion, not a heart attack. The doctor asked me if I had eaten anything unusual. I had to think about it. After the florist, I did wolf down three chili dogs. It looked like the all-American chili dog I had at the Greeks didn't agree with me. That's what it was.

When I finally told the doctor that my father just died and my mother and brother were out of the country, he suggested it would help if I could talk to a friend or a clergyman. He left the room to get the technician. Suddenly, the four white walls were closing in, caving in on me in slow motion. I yanked the EKG leads from my chest, slid off the examining table, and, in seconds, I was out the door. I escaped. I escaped so I could go home and break into my empty house, sink into the couch and watch my father's gray sweater draped over his reading chair.

I went from couch to chair, from room to room. Finally, I sat down in the empty kitchen. I imagined my father behind the steering wheel the moment he swerved the Chrysler into the tree. I visualized the violence of the impact, the shattered glass on the visor, my father gasping, choking on his dentures. Then I saw my father butt-naked, smoking in the kitchen in the wee hours of the morning, sitting exactly where I was sitting. It couldn't be. But it was. My father was gone.

I stood up and looked into the closet to find something I could wear for the funeral. My father's starched shirts hung painfully in the half-dark. I swallowed. The pain in my chest was back. A tightening noose that held my ribs together. I felt that if I let go I would some-how disintegrate, and I wouldn't be able to put my parts back together again. That no one could. Not my mother. Not my brother. Due to arrive only hours before the services were to begin at Bodnár & Sons on Saturday.

I contacted the minister at the Hungarian Lutheran Church on Denison Avenue, the one my father attended two or three times a year, only to fall asleep after making a grand entrance with his well-dressed family. I remembered how my Lutheran father and Catholic mother fought about religion. My mother was critical of the minis-ter's wife, who was also the organist, for wearing dresses that were too low-cut, too vulgar for a minister's wife. To this, my father retorted that at least they didn't have nuns in the Lutheran church. "Brides of Christ! How many brides was Christ supposed to have? A goddamm harem?"

No, talking to a clergyman would not help me at this juncture in my life. I was on my own. It was sink or swim time. I took a blue Compoz pill with a glass of water. I was still sitting in the dark kitchen at four in the morning, wearing nothing but my boxer shorts. I was puffing away on my father's cigarettes, staring blankly at the ancient Olivetti typewriter he left on the kitchen table. My father wasn't a writer, but he sure wrote a lot of letters. Letters to relatives in Hungary bragging about America's military superiority, letters to American politicians warning them about the latest Communist conspiracy, the "Red Menace," the "Cancer of Communism." Letters of admiration to the likes of General Walker and Governor Wallace.

Without exception my father saved a copy of every letter he had ever written. A habit, he called it. A hobby, a duty. For posterity.

I went through the box of his papers. Took me hours. I even examined the overflowing wastebasket in the kitchen. I never read any of my father's letters, and when he read from them, I was quick to leave the room. It was all garbage. But now something made me root through his garbage. I glanced at one or two crumpled sheets.

The beginnings of a letter to some Jewish society in New York. One or two lines, nothing more. A false start. Pieces of torn-up carbon paper. Scraps and shit. Of course copies of finished letters were tucked away in a safe along with important documents, bank books, etc., and only he and my mother knew the combination.

There was nothing much in the wastebasket this time. One empty envelope caught my attention because it was so weird. The way it was addressed. "The Heritage Vault Corporation c/o Brigadeführer Dr. Arthúr Kun."

Brigadeführer?!

I tossed it back into the wastebasket. Then sighed. My father's mind had gone AWOL.

I picked up the wastebasket and took it out to the garage and the incinerator. Trash-burning time.

The smell of burning paper brought back my part-time job in the Ars Medica building. I stared into the flames. Fire was good at making things go away. Tons of tormenting medical journals, my failing grades, all things seen and unseen.

A surge of freedom coursed through me. It was momentary only. The metal hatch got so hot I had to use the frigging poker. In the process, I discovered a neat row of empty wine bottles. Hidden behind the incinerator. My father must've concealed a dozen or so. So, the old man had been hitting the bottle. This much? And in such a short time? It wasn't long ago I tossed my failing report card into the fire.

I went back into the kitchen and looked under the sink. The last time I did that there were at least four full bottles. Now, nothing. The gallon jug of California wine my uncle usually drank when he wasn't doing his milk and *pálinka* cocktail was damn near empty.

Without knowing what I wanted I opened the fridge door and just stood there. The smell of moth balls hit my nose. Nothing but salami, salt pork, and old cheese. The whole fridge smelled of deodorizer. I had to smile. That was my father, alright. He still hadn't thrown out the urinal deodorizer. I decided I wasn't hungry. I poured myself what was left of the California wine, and the sour taste soon gave way to a calming warmth. I drowsed off right in the kitchen chair. I saw my father's body pass in front of me in my uncle's hearse. His waterlogged body was floating in a fiberglass vault, the skin on his head wrinkled into folds. My father's eyes were wide open. A procession of wailing women in black babushkas ran after a black hearse but there was no way of catching an American Eldorado. I was among the women, running in place, panting, holding my chest.

When I woke up, I fought off the tightness under my breastbone and stumbled to the bathroom. I washed my face with cold water. Christ, I was a wreck. I thought about calling up the police station to ask Sergeant Johnson about my father's alcohol level. I made a sour face in the mirror. Now, why would I do that? My father was not a drunk. Sure, he had an occasional drink like all good Hungarians. The problem was, he wasn't supposed to drink because of his health.

I felt the noose around my chest tighten when I opened my father's closet. I was surprised the first white shirt I tried on fit me to a T. My father had been trim not because he was fit, but because he was sickly, with a weak constitution and a weak spirit. I wondered if it was his weak spirit that drove him into the tree. A tug on the steering wheel is all it would take. Just a tug. Unless he was drunk out of his mind and lost control. That envelope with the *Brigadeführer* bullshit, what was that? He must've been bombed out of his gourd.

I didn't own a dark suit. A brown blazer and black slacks would have to do. As for shoes, the only thing black I owned were my shiny, ballroom shoes.

CHAPTER 11

"For I will take you away from among the nations, gather you from all foreign lands, and bring you back to your own land. I will sprinkle water upon you to cleanse you from all your impurities, and from all your idols I will cleanse you. I will give you a new heart and place a new spirit within you, taking from your bodies your stony hearts."

—(Ezekiel 36:24)

Me and Gypsy were the first to arrive at the funeral parlor. No sign yet of my mother and brother or anyone else. The chilly air in the parlor made the place smell like refrigerated carnations. The last time I saw so many folding chairs stenciled with Bodnár & Sons was at the meeting of the Lake Erie Soccer League. We signed the guest book and took a memorial card of Psalm 23. On the back were my father's dates and an obituary with mention of his doctorate degree and his appointment to the Royal Hungarian Bench.

Mr. Bodnár escorted us to my father's coffin. I had made a good choice. The imitation bronze looked real in the glow of the candles. A lighted gallery of flowers and wreaths and long stemmed gladiolas surrounded the coffin. My oversized cross of red, white, and green carnations stood out prominently from the others.

I was afraid to linger by my father just yet, and led Gypsy away from the coffin to another room. I told Gypsy I wanted him to see Joe. Joe was the guy next door, in a coffin. His memorial cards read Joseph Kaminsky. *Requiescat in pace.* A total stranger. He had a thick neck, and you could see the make-up smeared around his ear.

We went back to my father. My father looked better than in real life. His face seemed fuller on the ruffled pillow, his color almost ruddy, as if he had spent his life on the beach. Mr. Bodnár, or whoever did the embalming, had given him a tan. The shirt collar was still too large for his neck. The longish hands, the veins bulging with embalming fluid, were folded in prayer.

My Uncle Arthúr came up behind me and put a hand on my shoulder. "Where did the police say he hit his head?"

I shrugged because I really didn't know.

"Look on the left side," my uncle said. "By the hairline you can see where Bodnár filled it in."

I nodded.

My uncle said my mother and brother were here. I turned around. My mother, wearing a black suit, hat with veil, and my brother, in what looked like some tailored black suit were making their way toward me.

We embraced. The three of us stood awkwardly by the coffin until my mother crossed herself and turned around to greet the guests, most of them Hungarian refugees like us. What surprised me was that no one cried. Anna? Was she misty eyed or was it the light?

My mother and brother seemed more worn out than anything. She looked me up and down and sniffled. She said she appreciated the arrangements, although my father's wish was to be cremated. But never mind. Uncle Arthúr wanted to help out with the vault. "You know your uncle," she said. "Your father, he was a Christian first and foremost. Don't ever forget that, Attila." She reached into her purse, took out a handkerchief and dabbed her eyes. Then she handed me a twenty-dollar bill and told me to go to Thom McCann across the street and buy a pair of proper black shoes. What I had on were more appropriate for the dance floor than a father's funeral.

It shocked me that my father would want to be cremated. To be incinerated. Didn't make any sense. Wasn't it against all that he professed? His sensibility and all that? I realized how little I knew my father and how little he knew me. My mother's cruel remarks hurt me deeply. Her comment about my Hungarian floral cross. Something about me being a separatist. "Why not one wreath from the family? Oh, never mind."

Outside, it got suddenly cold. Only in Cleveland can weather turn nasty just like that. And nasty it was. Green leaves blew every which way against a dark horizon. The wind whipped up the dust in the parking lot.

The caravan to Holy Cross Cemetery was hastily organized in what was becoming a hailstorm. Tornado weather. Mr. Bodnár's black Cadillac, bearing the body, led the caravan, followed by Uncle Arthúr's Eldorado with my mother, brother and myself. A dozen or so cars followed. We were given instructions to keep our headlights on. The little blue "Funeral" flag tacked to each car ended up taking a real beating from the marble-sized hail. At one point, our motorcycle escort had to pull under a bridge.

The Eldorado's wipers were in high gear, and ice was caking on the edges of the windshield. It was the most freakish hailstorm on record. In a matter of a few minutes the white stuff covered everything in sight. My mother and uncle sat up front, me and my brother in the back. My uncle was the first to speak. "It was his eyesight. His eyesight let him down."

My mother said: "He shouldn't have been driving. The man had no reflexes. But he insisted."

"It was a power thing with him," my uncle said. "Some men think that pushing on the accelerator makes them powerful. Potent."

"What are we going to do now?" my mother said.

My uncle said, "We're going to give him a proper Christian burial. And then we're going to pool our resources and start anew. That's what we're all about." He looked into the rearview. "That's what this country's all about."

My response was that I didn't want to go to medical school anymore. My brother surprised everybody by saying the same thing.

"You don't have to," my mother said. "We need all the help we can get. You're going to have a bright future. That I will see to. Your father had accidental-death insurance in the amount of $10,000. Not a lot of money, mind you. But enough to give you each a share in your uncle's business."

Uncle Arthúr's eyes appeared in the rearview again. He was trying to gauge my reaction. There was none. I looked outside the window at the incredible mantle of ice on the grass. My brother, on the other hand, was all for it. Keeping the money in the family was a pretty smart thing to do, as far as he was concerned. Anything else was stupid.

Holy Cross Cemetery looked more like a snow-covered golf course than a cemetery. I guessed that the reason all the headstones were level with the ground was to make it easier to mow the lawn. My father was to be buried in the non-Catholic section, and his headstone would have to come later. In spite of all the money we were pooling together as a family, it looked like we couldn't afford a headstone for my father. Something about cash flow.

The wind was still gusting. The cold humid air mixed with smoke from the steel mills and from the Ford Brookpark Plant nearby.

Half the old soccer team came to the funeral including Jakab Rosenberg. My crazy old man was right for once. Jakab's last name *was* Rosenberg. I was surprised to see him since he really wasn't part of the team. He only played in that one game. Professor Robert Oszlányi was among the mourners. The professor was shaking the ice from his umbrella. Dr. Losonczy was there, too. Endre Szabó and his wife were holding on to each other, to brave the cold gusts that were finding their way under the green canopy. Mr. Gayer, the florist, was there with his beautiful, alcoholic wife, but the minister's wife was conspicuously absent.

My father's gravesite was a few feet from the curb. The wind knocked over the gladiolas in their plastic vases. A long-stemmed flower landed on the concrete.

I was standing with family and friends under the flapping canvas when I noticed Millie in her blue raincoat. She was standing by one of the aluminum posts holding up the canopy, her black hair blowing in the wind.

The minister hurried: "Ashes to ashes. Dust to dust." He sprinkled holy water on the bronze coffin as it was lowered into a Heritage vault, which was quickly sealed with epoxy and lowered further still into the open grave. A flower or two fell on the fiberglass cover, shaped like a submarine hull.

The small knot of mourners commended the soul of Dr. Ferenc Nagy to his Creator.

> *Into Your hands we commend our spirit, O Lord.*
> *Into Your hands we commend our hearts.*

The gravesite ceremony was cut short because of the brutal wind and the cold. It couldn't have been a drearier day for a funeral. My mother saw Millie and went out of her way to tell me the wake for my father was for family only.

Uncle Arthúr gave me the keys to his Eldorado and told me to bring the car around for my mother.

I took the keys.

My eyes were following Millie. She was walking toward her mother's convertible.

I fired up the Eldorado and stepped on the gas. I came to a screeching stop by Millie as she was about to open her car door. The electric window came down. "Get in!" I said. It sounded like an order.

"What?"

"Please, Millie. Just get in."

She got in. "What's going on?"

"We're getting the hell out of here," I said.

I floored it. A tug on the power steering and the Eldorado jumped the curb. I took out one of the aluminum posts holding up the green canopy. The canvas collapsed on the fiberglass vault.

Endre Szabó had to dive to avoid being run over. Uncle Arthúr shook a fist, mouthed obscenities.

I was a barbarian motherfucker and I knew it.

The Eldorado careened out of control over hollowed ground, then with a jerk fishtailed onto the slippery asphalt.

We zoomed by the cemetery gate, missing it by inches. Millie was screaming. I continued at neck-breaking speeds on Brookpark Road, running the first red light. Then I slowed down to sixty, but by that time Millie was frantic. "You're crazy. You're going to get us killed. Where, where are we going?"

I had no idea so I just said Florida.

Strangely, that seemed to satisfy her, and she settled back. "Would you slow down, please. We'd like to arrive alive."

I shot her a look. "I love you, Millie," I said.

"I never stopped loving you."

In the rearview I spotted Gypsy's red Fastback. The Mustang quickly caught up to my bumper. Gypsy was giving me the thumbs up. It meant go, man, go.

And we went.

We kept driving and driving in my uncle's stolen hearse. The further south the better. We took back roads through Ohio, Kentucky. Two more states and we'd be hitting sunny Florida. It seemed like every time I blinked I was checking the rearview. Millie kept asking if we were being followed. I replied, "Not yet."

Millie had some pictures to show me. She slid these glossy black and whites from her bag. Pictures her father's private detective had taken of the two of us by the Art Museum. The man in the tree wasn't a pervert after all. Or maybe he was. But the real pervert, Millie said, was her father. No way would she ever go back to him.

"You're with me now," I said.

We were going to start a new life. Just the two of us. *We* were family. The two of us. We were going to leave behind the cruel weather and our cruel past. We were going to leave behind the Terminal Tower and the whole stinking, polluted city. Abused by all the stinking steel mills corporate America was spewing in the air. We were going to leave behind the goddamm grand familia.

Somewhere around Lexington, Kentucky, during one of our pit stops, my fingers found something when I reached for my pack of cigarettes in the Eldorado's door. I was stunned to see what I pulled out. The same medical advisory I once translated for my father. The same WARNING printed in large bold letters. About drinking alcohol and eating certain foods while taking a certain medication. What was this doing in my uncle's car? What else was in the Eldorado? In the glove compartment?

Like a madman, I rummaged through the glove compartment. I swept aside a crushed styrofoam cup, an owner's manual, insurance papers and shit. Tons of Heritage Vault brochures. Buried underneath was an envelope addressed to my uncle the *Brigadeführer* in care of his business. I recognized the Olivetti type. Inside was a letter from my father. My father was demanding money. Lots of money. Otherwise he'd turn incriminating documents over to the authorities. The New York Jewish Refugee Aid Society, the Nokmim League, the FBI, the CIA, etc, etc. Christ, the old man was blackmailing my uncle and the sonofobitch killed him! I knew about mixing booze with the meds. I just knew! The sonofabitch knew, too!

Christ Almighty! I told Millie, and it didn't take her long to figure out where I was coming from. We were on the road already when I pounded my fist on the dash. I should've done something, but what? Should've. Could've. There was no end to it. The guilt. The anxiety.

The paranoia. I was anxious to leave all that shit behind if I was to make a clean break with the past. Let the freaking dead bury the dead.

"It's not your fault," Millie said. "And you're not paranoid. If you want me to, I can make an anonymous call to the Fairview cops. You can always mail a photocopy of what you found. Otherwise, you'll spend your life torturing yourself about it."

"No. This is something I need to do myself."

When we pulled into the next service station, I tanked up, bought some chips, Hostess Cupcakes and a thermos of coffee, and I made the call.

"Did they say anything about the car?" Millie asked, once I was behind the wheel again.

"No. The sonofobitch owes me."

"You can't keep it, you know."

"I don't want to keep it. I'm just using it to get us the hell out of there."

I realized I was escaping. Again. I felt my chest tighten another notch. It was the old noose. There was no escape this time. I felt like I was going to get sick or cry. My eyes blurred, but I was determined not to cave in. Christ. What is it with me?

I had to pull off the road to pull myself together. Millie held me. We held each other. She said it was okay. Okay to let it out.

I was unraveling. The tight noose holding my ribs and my insides together was coming undone. A floodgate opened. I sobbed. My chest heaved violently. I sobbed until it was all out and I could breathe again. Breathe freely. Like I was given a new heart. Millie's eyes filled with tears. Our eyes locked. Only her eyes could take me in like that, and I knew in that instant that the warmth I felt when Millie looked at me would always be enough.

We fell asleep holding each other. It was only when the darkness and the fog lifted that we were able to make out the sign "Scenic Lookout."

I rolled down the window. A light sprinkle. We were high up somewhere in the Smoky Mountains. Below us a valley of shiny housetops glinted in the sun. God's valley. It was early morning. We had the last of the coffee from the thermos, still hot and still good.

We were singing, I was drumming on the dash, I was reciting poetry to her. We drove through the mountains, up spruce covered peaks, down narrow country roads where we whipped up the dust. It was warm enough to keep the windows down and dangle out an arm. Even horse dung smelled sweet.

It was as if my life began with Millie.

We drove through the red earth of Georgia, and once we crossed the state line came the bright blue sky, the white, open highways of Florida. And we kept going south on A1A along sand dunes and palm trees—and the vast, endless, blue-green ocean.

EPILOGUE

Millie Weiler and Attila Nagy have been married going on 40 years now, their union blessed with two children and five grandchildren.

As for the Eldorado, it found a final resting place in a deep canal on the fringes of the Florida Everglades where it has been submerged for the last four decades. The last Millie and Attila saw of his uncle's hearse was its bumper sticker as it went under—*Undertakers Do It Last*. Its owner, Arthúr Kun, was found guilty of murder in the death of his brother-in-law, Ferenc Nagy. After serving out his twenty-year sentence in the Ohio State Penitentiary, Kun was arraigned on a separate charge and convicted by the United States government for "Crimes Against Humanity." Below is an excerpt of the Count One charge:

1. Between October, 1944, and March, 1945, the defendant herein committed Crimes against Humanity as defined by Control Council Law No. 10 in that he was principal and accessory to atrocities and offenses, including but not limited to murder, extermination, enslavement, deportation, persecution on political, racial and religious grounds.

2. Kidnapping the children of foreign nationals who were considered to have "racial value."

3. Encouraging and compelling abortions on Eastern European workers for the purpose of preserving their working capacity as slave labor.

4. Preventing marriages and hampering reproduction of "enemy" nationals.

5. Participating in the persecution and extermination of Jews.

About the Author

Peter Hargitai is an award-winning translator, poet and novelist. His selection of the poems of Attila József in *Perched on Nothing's Branch* garnered for him the Academy of American Poets Landon Translation Award and a listing among world classics in Harold Bloom's *The Western Canon.* For his translation of Antal Szerb's novel *The Traveler,* he was awarded the Füst Milán Prize from the Hungarian Academy of Sciences; and for his steadfast commitment to translating, publishing, and teaching Hungarian literature in a world language, he was awarded the Pro Cultura Hungarica Medal from the Republic of Hungary. Professor Hargitai is on the English faculty at Florida International University.

978-0-595-39920-8
0-595-39920-7

Printed in the United States
74324LV00006B/213